Catching Raven
Volume II

CB Tucker

Author's Tranquility Press
ATLANTA, GEORGIA

Copyright © 2024 by CB Tucker

All rights reserved. No part of this publication may be reproduced, distributed or transmitted in any form or by any means, including photocopying, recording, or other electronic or mechanical methods, without the prior written permission of the publisher, except in the case of brief quotations embodied in critical reviews and certain other noncommercial uses permitted by copyright law. For permission requests, write to the publisher, addressed "Attention: Permissions Coordinator," at the address below.

CB Tucker / Author's Tranquility Press
3900 N Commerce Dr. Suite 300 #1255
Atlanta, GA 30344, USA
www.authorstranquilitypress.com

Ordering Information:
Quantity sales. Special discounts are available on quantity purchases by corporations, associations, and others. For details, contact the "Special Sales Department" at the address above.

Catching Raven / CB Tucker
Paperback: 978-1-964362-87-8
eBook: 978-1-964037-69-1

PREFACE

When we left, Samantha was loaded onto a plane with Elizabeth, and Jamie explained that they were flying to another store. It wasn't until they left the runway on the Plantation that she was informed that the store was in Paris, France.

This left Samantha in shock, since the only clothing she had that belonged to her, was her shoes. She had no money, no passport, and no clothes to change into. She also didn't know where they would be sleeping. For a woman who just gained control of her life, this predicament was disturbing.

She was plagued by uncertainty. Can Trevor Paterson do this? Then again, Trevor Paterson can do this and conquer numerous other obstacles. Because of this wealth, his potential is astounding. However, he is not the type of man who abuses the privileges that his wealth affords him.

Sam has been transplanted into Trevor's world. In Trevor's world, the friends are many, but the enemies are countless. Danger lurks around every corner, and vigilance is paramount. Every day brings new friends, new enemies, and new challenges.

Sam will now have to reach deep down into her core to carry herself through the new onslaught of problems and challenges that lie ahead. Can she and Elizabeth deal with what is now coming? Only time will tell.

She will encounter more problems, and new challenges, and people who were friends will become enemies. She has more questions than answers. How wealthy is Trevor? Does he even know? Does he want

Samantha back into his life or only Elizabeth? What are his plans for her?

Can she continue living in Winder, GA, or will he demand she move to the Plantation? Can she work at the Hutchinson Accounting Firm, or is that even possible? What are his plans for Elizabeth? She needs help dealing with the traumatic experience of Jimmy Dittle. Where is Jimmy Dittle and his crew, and what happened to Roger Dawson and his compatriots?

But first, she is going to have to deal with arriving in Paris France with no documents, no clothes, and no toothbrush in Trevor's hideous Guayabera shirt.

Then there is the question of Jamie and Susan. Who are they? What were those badges they were showing? How can they do what they do? Sam sank back into the comfortable, overstuffed chair with a pounding headache caused by all the questions and strain on her mind, body, and soul.

Her thoughts were interrupted by an inquiry. "You look like a woman with questions. Why don't you try one?"

Sam looked at the catty woman sitting across from her with a knowing smile. She owed them for what they had done for her. At this very moment, she loved them, and she hated them. And yes, she had questions.

CHAPTER 1:
A trip to Paris

As the Gulf Stream climbed to altitude, the ladies sat back in their plush leather seats that resembled lazy boy recliners, facing each other separated only by a table. Samantha was curled up in her seat messaging her temples for the headache that was pounding away. Jamie and Susan sat across from Sam and Liz, studying them after they received the sudden news of the unscheduled trip to Paris. Jamie looked at Samantha, "Headache?"

Sam opened her eyes and glared at both Jamie and Susan. Jamie started to chuckle, and Susan asked, "You look like a woman with questions, so try one."

Sam looked at both women and dropped her hands into her lap in desperation. "Yes, I do. Why are we making this trip?"

Jamie gave her a smile. "I told you Trevor called me and was upset that you hadn't spent more. He needed to get the two of you out of the country, so here we are."

Sam glanced at Liz then back at the women. "Do you know why he wanted us out of the country?"

Jamie shook her head no. "We will find out when we return, but until then, we get a free shopping trip in Paris."

Sam nodded. "You showed badges at the hotel---are the two of you police?"

Susan spoke up first. "I was Atlanta Police for ten years then an MMA fighter. Jamie was Army then Delta as well as Army Police, but the Badges are from the State Department."

Sam gave both women a confused look. "State Department, I don't understand?"

Jamie smiled and replied, "At every Embassy or consulate, there is a person called the Regional Security Officer. They oversees the security of the facility and is sort of the U.S. Sheriff of that facility. They have limited jurisdiction in that country and the U.S., but most people only look at the badge."

Sam and Liz glanced at each other. Sam allowed her head to fall back against the seat and closed her eyes for a second, trying to wrap her brain around this new information. A voice behind her spoke asking, "Would any of you like refreshment?" Sam jumped almost out of her seat and looked behind her at the beautiful female stewardess standing there.

Susan chuckled. "We would like a glass of wine."

Jamie smiled, in the spirit of their trip to France, she replied, "Bordeaux, please."

Susan smiled and said, "Two."

Liz sat up and drank in the scene. She looked at her mother and asked," Can I have one Mom? We would be enjoying some red wine on the couch right now if we were at home."

Jamie chuckled and retorted, "So we have a cultured girl here, do we?"

Sam looked over her shoulder and nodded. "Make it four." She looked at Jamie and Susan and added, "We have a glass of wine while we read, talk, and unwind in the evening." The stewardess nodded and left to pour the wine. Sam looked back at the two women across from her. "Trevor admitted he put cameras in my house, tapped my phone, and put a GPS on me. I want to know who and why?"

Susan and Jamie looked at each other before Jamie said, "Correction, we put the cameras in, the phone tap, and the GPS tracker in your house and on you."

Samantha looked at both women with hurt on her face. "I trusted you, and you violated my trust." Susan sat forward but then stopped as the stewardess returned with their wine.

Susan waited for her to leave then leaned back forward and replied, "Sam, yes, we did violate your trust, but please consider why we did it. If we didn't have those cameras, we would not have gotten a lead on Jasper Grebes. We wouldn't have been able to listen in on that phone conversation with Jimmy Dittle, and we wouldn't have known where you were. Look, we are sorry, but we did have our reasons."

Sam took a sip of wine and looked intently at both women. "Yes, hacking into my life like that did aid you in saving Liz and me, but what if Jimmy hadn't kidnapped Liz? And what if Roger had not blackmailed me into . . ." Sam paused for a moment. "And why didn't Trevor just come out and tell me? Why did he have to violate my privacy before coming forward?"

Susan and Jamie glanced at each other and chuckled. Jamie leaned forward and explained, "The reason Trevor asked for your help was because he wanted to meet you. Morgenstern International is a subsidiary of Paterson Global, and they reported two remarkable women in Atlanta doing outstanding work. The description matched your profile. When we talked to Mr. Bushier from the bank about you, Trevor became very interested. We watched you for two weeks before deciding to move forward."

Sam looked at Jamie and Susan in shock and started to speak when Jamie interjected. "Trevor has been looking for you for some time, but when we investigated you, we noticed some unfavorable characters making a habit of immersing themselves in your life. He was worried and asked if we would take steps to ensure your safety. As for revealing himself to you, we advised him to, but he was scared that you would reject him before he could explain."

Liz started to say something, but Sam sat forward and asked, "So that whole thing was staged---he didn't need my help?"

Susan smiled. "No, he had already come to the same conclusion as yours, but when you came up with an analysis in less than a week, well, there were some bent egos here."

Liz chimed in with questions of her own. "Do you work for the State Department?"

Susan looked at Jamie and replied, "No, but because of Trevor's work, they use us to talk to people they can't access. Sometimes Trevor can come in and work a deal that they can't, and because of that, they allow us to use these badges."

Liz became excited. "So, you work with the HLS, CIA, and all those alphabet types?"

Jamie chuckled then looked forward before replying, "Well, I can't say what we do---this place is not secure, but yes, we assist our government in many ways from time to time."

Jamie saw Liz yawn and interjected, "Look, we are going to arrive in Paris, France just before eight in the morning. Now I'm not sure how long we will have, but I don't intend to waste time sleeping. We should try to get some rest." Sam nodded in agreement and reclined in her seat. Jamie sat up and looked directly at Sam. "Sam, before you get mad at Trevor for what we did, consider this: I have known him for ten years, and I know for a fact that he is a good man. Everything he does is for a reason, and normally, we agree with his choices in the end."

She glanced at Susan and continued, "As for that blow-up in his office, we wouldn't have missed that show for anything in the world." Sam looked down at her hands trying to figure out if blowing up like that was good or bad.

Susan chuckled and said, "Hear, hear." Sam gave them a pensive smile.

The stewardess came over to retrieve the glasses and deliver some blankets. Soon the lights dimmed, and the four ladies curled up with the blankets to sleep. At seven-thirty in the morning, the jet landed on a private airstrip just outside of Paris. They taxied over to the vehicles waiting, and an officer from French immigration boarded the plane and started checking the passports of Susan and Jamie.

Sam looked at Liz, and fear gripped her. She didn't have a passport, a change of clothes, or even a toothbrush! She watched as the shopping bags were carried off, and the tall immigration officer walked over to Sam. In a heavy French accent, he asked, "Your papers, Madame?"

Sam retrieved her driver's license from her wallet and handed it to the officer. The officer took the card and looked at both sides then back at Sam. "What is this?"

Sam gave a weak smile and replied, "I'm sorry, but I didn't know I was coming. So…I didn't grab my passport, did I say I'm sorry."

The officer looked angry. "So, you do have a passport?"

Sam was wringing her hands as she continued to sit on the edge of the seat with her weak smile. She glanced at Susan and Jamie before she replied, "Well no, I don't have one."

The officer shook his head and sighed. He turned his attention to Liz. "Mademoiselle, do you have your documents?" Liz gave a weak smile and handed him her library card. The officer looked at the card and then back at Jamie and Susan, who were standing with smirks near the door. They were still in their exercise outfits. He turned back to the two ladies seated before him.

The officer put his hands on his hips and barked, "So what makes you think you can come to France without the proper documents? What are you here for?"

Liz squeaked out a reply, "We need to buy some clothes."

The officer looked at Sam, who was still wearing Trevor's Guayabera shirt. "That I see. Is that all you came here to do?"

Jamie spoke up. "Hit some clubs, drink, eat, and party."

The officer turned and looked at her then back at Liz. "You are what . . . fifteen?"

Liz glanced at her mother and then up at the officer before nodding yes. The officer nodded slowly in return and studied her for a few seconds. "My daughter is now fifteen, and if it wasn't for Mr. Paterson, she wouldn't have made it."

He handed Sam and Liz back their cards. "Welcome to Paris, and please, once you get your new clothes, burn that! "He pointed at Trevor's shirt.

Sam gave him a hurt look and replied, "It belongs to Trevor, and I just borrowed it." The officer turned then stopped and looked back at Samantha, and said, "I will not ask why you are wearing his clothes, but Knowing monsieur Paterson as I do, I can only imagine." He walked towards Jamie and Susan. He handed them his card and retorted, " Call me when you go to the club." He exited the airplane.

Jamie and Susan glanced back at Sam and Liz and smiled at them. Sam stood up, straightened Trevor's shirt, and motioned for Liz to come. They walked proudly to the front of the plane to exit. They entered the limousine, and in a few minutes, they arrived at another mansion. Sam exited the vehicle and gawked at the large, gothic building.

Sam allowed her eyes to climb the walls of the beautiful building and looked back at her daughter. "Let's hope they have a toothbrush."

CHAPTER 2:
The fun begins

The girls slowly entered the foyer. They were absorbing the grandeur of the mansion when Maurice greeted them. He was a thin man who stood about six feet tall. He donned a three-piece, gray suit. He approached Jamie and kissed her on both cheeks along with Susan, but he appeared to be nervous around Susan. Susan shot him a condescending look. "Have you been behaving, Maurice?"

Maurice stepped back nervously. "But! Of course."

He turned to Sam and Liz. "Let's see what we have here! Ah yes, pretty, very pretty, but that is a hideous dress! You should not be caught dead in that, but I think we can work with this. Now I suggest that we show you to your rooms so you can freshen up. We have an appointment at 1 pm?"

One of the servants came into the foyer with two duffel bags, and Maurice ordered, "Put those in their rooms," as he pointed at Jamie and Susan.

Sam looked at the bags, "Wait, you have luggage!?"

Jamie chuckled. "We have emergency luggage that was placed onto the aircraft before we arrived."

Sam sneered haughtily at Jamie. "So, you have clothes, and I'm stuck in this?"

Susan replied, "We would offer you an outfit, but I don't think they will fit." Sam crossed her arms and tapped her foot as she looked at both women with disdain.

Jamie chuckled again. "We have toothbrushes." Sam stepped forward with her hand out. Jamie opened the side pocket of her bag, removed two spare toothbrushes, and handed them to Sam. Once she and Liz received their toothbrushes, they all retired to their rooms.

The ladies showered, and Sam was relieved to find that she did have some fresh underwear, which was part of the purchases they made in Winder before leaving. The problem was that now the only thing she had to wear was Trevor's damned Guayabera shirt! This shirt had quickly become the bane of her sartorial existence. Sam lay down for a while before sliding back into the wretched shirt and heading downstairs.

Several hours later, all four women were back down in the foyer. Susan and Jamie were now wearing nice dresses, and Sam sucked her teeth at them in disgust. Liz appeared wearing the dress that she and her mother were arguing about before leaving. Sam gaped at the dress. Jamie smiled. "Remember who is paying for it."

Sam heaved a sigh and gave Jamie a look of dismay. "I hope that man is worth all of this." Jamie and Susan could barely contain the snickers that threatened to burst from their mouths.

Maurice approached the ladies. "Come, come, we have an appointment with Louis Vuitton." A stretch limousine sat out front, and Maurice waited for the four ladies to enter before he joined them. They were on their way!

It took another hour for them to arrive at large a showroom just a few blocks from the Arc de Triomphe on Les Champs-Elysées. As they entered the showroom, Maurice led the way and introduced them to the current designer in charge, Nicolas Ghesquiere. Nicolas was a dashing gentleman in his forties, just under six feet with dark hair and piercing gray eyes. Nicolas greeted Maurice with a hug and a kiss on both cheeks and did the same to Jamie and Susan. Nicolas turned to look at Samantha, placed both hands on his hips, and began to assess her

Samantha stared helplessly at her daughter, Jamie, and Susan as if she were being appraised like a horse at auction. She looked down at herself and back at Nicolas with trepidation. After Nicolas circled, her he snapped his fingers to summon his assistant. "This is the raw subject of my canvas. Let's see, one fifty-three tall, two forty kilos, eighty-one, sixty-six, ninety-one, nice face with a hideous choice of clothes. What do you call this...look?"

He pointed at the shirt Sam was wearing. Sam glanced at Susan and Jamie in frustration and responded defiantly, "Excuse me, but this is not my shirt. I borrowed it." Nicolas was relaying instructions to his young, female assistant when he heard Sam. He turned slowly and retorted, "Give it back--- it is horrible this way. We need to make you look like a woman." Sam vowed then and there, that she would never wear this shirt again, not even to run to Trevor's kitchen for a late-night snack.

Sam looked at Jamie and Susan, who were doing their best to squelch their laughter and shook her head in disgust. Jamie gave her a nudge with her shoulder, "Come on, this is where it gets fun." Sam followed Jamie into a small theater with a walkway extending out from some curtains about twenty feet long and raised about two feet above the floor. The rest of the room was dark, and the lights in the ceiling all focused on the walkway.

Susan and Liz sat together, and Jamie sat with Sam on one side of the walkway while Nicolas was sitting on the other side with several assistants. The first model emerged from the curtains. Sam admired the fashion, but it wasn't her style. She leaned over to Jamie and asked, "So how does this work?"

Jamie replied, "When you see something you like, just nod."

Sam looked at her for a second and asked, "But how do I pay?"

"You're with Trevor now. He will foot the bill, and tomorrow morning, the outfits you choose will be at the mansion fully tailored."

Samantha raised an eyebrow and focused on the next model walking down the ramp--- it still wasn't her style. The next model appeared in a beautiful dress, and Sam nodded. Nicolas spoke to an assistant who exited, and another assistant took her place. This continued until the four women picked twenty-five outfits. Sam picked eight, while Liz picked ten. Susan and Jamie picked the rest.

As they were leaving, Nicolas approached Sam and asked in a heavy French accent, "Madame, if you don't mind, would you please leave in this?" Sam looked at him and then at his assistant, who held up a gray pantsuit with a lavender silk blouse and undergarments.

Sam started to ask why when Susan leaned over and whispered, "Sam, he can't afford to allow you to leave here in that." Sam looked down at Trevor's shirt and back at Nicolas. She knew Susan was correct. If Sam were seen leaving Louis Vuitton in a Guayabera shirt, it would spread all over town in two hours. Sam nodded, allowing the assistant to guide her to a changing room where she transformed.

When she exited the changing room, Samantha looked like a different woman. She had finally discarded Trevor's shirt. She walked over to Jamie and Susan, but now she wore an 800-dollar, silk pants suit, and no longer had to wear that nightmare of a shirt. Jamie chuckled. "Don't you like getting even with Trevor this way?"

Sam smiled and turned to Nicolas. "What is the damage?"

Nicolas turned to one of his assistants and showed her the bill. He replied, "It is 43.526,35 Euros, which is around 47,500 dollars."

Sam smiled and as she was leaving, whispered to Jamie, "Almost $48,000, and I'm wearing an $800 pantsuit with a thong. I have never worn a thong! I'm not the thong type. This will require some getting used to." Jamie choked another chuckle.

Maurice cleared his throat. "We are not done, ladies, and we have another appointment."

Liz smiled and asked, "Where to now?"

Maurice grinned. "How you say in America--- the beauty parlor. I have appointments for all of you at David Mallett in one hour, so we need to hurry." After David Mallett, they hit another French designer and returned to the chalet.

They made two more shopping trips on Saturday and hit several clubs. The customs agent suddenly appeared with his wife. On Monday and Tuesday, they continued to make the rounds of the designers.

Meanwhile, back at the Plantation on Tuesday, three vans approached the gates as the vehicle barrier lowered to allow them entrance. When they pulled to a stop before the mansion, several servants exited the building to retrieve the bags and carry them to their rooms on the second floor.

Thirty minutes later, the leaders of the party, along with two local security men, were in Trevor's office standing around the large table, looking at a map of the Plantation. Trevor pointed to the main gate. "He will of course approach here and attempt to gain access."

Jeff nodded. "He will be in one vehicle, but if he does bring a SWAT team as you suspect, they will have to come in two more vehicles." They worked out a plan of defense, and Jeff along with the two-squad leaders exited to prepare for the next day's events.

At 11 am on the following day, eight men exited the mansion in full camouflage and split into two groups. Each group had two men armed with AR-15s, and two of the men carried gas-powered dart rifles. Each group took their positions in the forest and waited for instructions via radio. At 1:15 pm, three vehicles approached the main entrance; and were greeted by two men dressed in black.

Trevor had built a pull-off to allow vehicles to pull off before turning into the Plantation. Beside the road was a sidewalk allowing the guard to approach the passenger side of the vehicle.

As the vehicles pulled to the side of the road, one man in black approached the passenger side of the vehicle. The window lowered, and the man sitting inside ordered, "I'm Captain Fletcher, and I have an appointment with Mr. Paterson. Lower the barrier, and let us in."

The man peered into the vehicle and asked, "ID?" The captain started to say something, and the guard interrupted. "Without ID, I won't allow you to enter." The captain pulled his credentials, collected the credentials from the other two, and handed them to the guard. The guard ordered, "Please lower the rear windows." The captain started to protest, but the guard held up his palm towards the captain and closed it quickly into a fist. The message was clear to anyone with military training--- shut up.

The lowered window revealed one detective in the back seat, and the other one was driving. The guard who returned the credentials held up a hand with one finger raised, turned to the captain, and said, "Only this vehicle will be allowed to enter." The captain smirked, waved, and led this driver forward. Just as his vehicle pulled out, the guard stepped behind it and in front of the second, causing a delay between the two. The barrier lowered, allowing the vehicle with the captain to enter. But before the second vehicle could push past the guard, the barrier went back up. The second and third vehicles stopped for a second and sped down the road away from the entrance.

Trevor lurked in the control room with Gary and the drone pilot. He looked over at the pilot and asked, "Got 'em?" The pilot nodded as he monitored the controls. "Gary ready for the first coordinates?" They watched as the second vehicle pulled to the side of the road, and the pilot called the coordinates out to Gary, who immediately relayed the numbers to the first group with a radio. A few minutes later, the second vehicle pulled over, and the pilot relayed those numbers to Gary, who called them into the second group.

The pilot circled back around to the first vehicle that pulled to the side, and they could see four men exit the vehicle, donning their gear. Gary radioed the new information to the groups.

The first group of four men suited up in their vests, armed with AR-15s, pistols, and knives before disappearing into the forest. It was now 1:45 pm, and the heat of the day was peaking. Clad in black, they pushed their way into the foliage and progressed about twenty feet before being stopped by a tall fence with coiled, barbed wire on the top. The leader of the group motioned for one of his men to approach the fence. The man started to cut the wire.

CHAPTER 3:
Swat vs. France

The SWAT member pulled a wire cutter and approached the fence. Before he could cut the wire, a voice sounded from the other side of the fence. They looked up, and there stood a man in a ghillie suit with a silenced AR-15 and scope standing glaring at them. The leader of the SWAT team looked at the man standing on the other side and commanded, "What did you say?"

The man repeated, "I wouldn't do that."

The leader chuckled and asked, "Who's going to stop us?"

The man retorted, "You will find that out if you come through the fence."

The leader shot back, "I suggest that you get the hell out of the way before we run over your ass."

The man chortled. "Okay, but there is a sign on the fence, and I just warned you. So, consider yourselves duly warned." The SWAT team chuckled as they looked at each other, but when they turned back, he was gone.

A Ghillie Suit is a misspelling of the term Gille. This is a reference to Gille Dubh a dark-haired lad who is sometimes called Earth Sprit. He is clothed in leaves and moss in Scottish mythology so he can hide. The Suite is designed to hide the wearer by blending into the environment. It is a favorite among snipers and Special Forces who are attempting to hide their presence. Soldiers wearing this camouflage have reported that people walked over them when they were wearing this suit.

The man shrugged his shoulders and then started to cut the fence, and in short order, there was an opening large enough to squeeze through. Two men held the fence open, and a third man stepped through. The man who had stepped through grabbed one side and held it open for the second man to follow, but just as the second man attempted to enter, a dart slammed into the first man's leg. The man yelped and looked down to pull the dart out when a dart slammed into the second man's leg.

The third man had just breached the opening when the second man was hit along with the third man. The first man dropped to the ground, followed closely by the other two men. The fourth man was still standing on the other side of the fence when he heard the voice again. "Go ahead and step through. I dare you."

The fourth man couldn't see where the voice was coming from and asked, "If I do, what will happen?"

"You need to ask?"

"Can I just leave?"

"You can leave if you want to, but you remember---I did warn the others."

The fourth man nodded, "Can I get the keys from that man right there?" The man from before appeared and pulled the keys from the identified SWAT member. He handed them to the last SWAT member. The last person took the keys, nodded, and then walked back out of the forest. As he was leaving, he pulled up his cell and made a call.

The same thing happened to the second team, only all four men had come through the fence. Soon, a man showed up with an ATV and a trailer. They loaded the men onto the trailer and left. When they picked up the second team, they found the keys to the SUV, and one man drove it around and into the Plantation. A crew arrived to repair the fence.

Amidst all this chaos, the captain's SUV pulled into a parking spot. As the captain exited the vehicle, one of the two guards at the front of the house stopped him. "No guns allowed sir." The captain stopped and gave him a disgusted look, glanced at the two detectives with him, and walked back to the vehicle. He opened the back, and they tossed their weapons in. Meanwhile, the captain received a phone call from the SWAT team member who chose not to come through the fence.

Captain Fletcher listened to what happened and yelled, "What do you mean they were taken out? What about team two?" He looked at the guard standing closest, who was armed with a side arm and an AR-15. "What happened to my SWAT teams?"

The guard shook his head. "I'm sure Mr. Paterson can tell you---this way." He followed the guard to the door, but instead of going in, the guard stepped to one side several feet away as the other guard backed into the foyer. Once the captain and his detectives entered the foyer, they found tables blocking them in, and the only way out was through a walk-through metal detector.

The captain looked at his detectives, and as he walked through the metal detector, an alarm sounded. He had to remove his keys, his change, and his ankle pistol before he made it through the WTMD. The same thing happened to both detectives, and they had to leave their ankle pistols on the table. When they tried to pick them up, they were gone. The tailing guard had already grabbed them.

The guard backed away. "Follow me, please." The three policemen glanced at each other and reluctantly followed the guard down the hall towards Trevor's office. The other guard tailed them just a few feet behind. When they reached Trevor's door, the lead guard entered first.

As the three policemen entered the office, the guard motioned towards the three chairs at the table. The guard turned to Trevor, "Both SWAT teams have been dealt with, sir."

The captain leered at the guard before eyeing Trevor, "What did you do to my SWAT teams?!"

Trevor was sitting at his desk with his elbows on the arms of his chair. His forearms rose to a pinnacle created by his fingers, pressed to his chin. He silently intimidated the three police officers. The guard motioned again for them to sit. Trevor sighed as he stared at the captain. "We haven't met, Captain Fletcher, but I can tell from your condescending attitude that you're an asshole and not used to following orders. Take serious heed---if you fail to do as I say again, the repercussions will be grave."

The three men glanced at each other and back at Trevor as Trevor rose from the desk and picked up four file folders. He advanced towards the three men. The captain leaned back in his chair as if to maintain his authoritative posture, but he only succeeded in fumbling his words, "Mr. Paterson, I'm not sure if you understand the situation, you have placed yourself in . . ."

Trevor abruptly dropped all four folders onto the table in front of the captain. "I know exactly what I'm doing, and more importantly, I know who the three of you are."

The three men glanced at each other. The captain started to speak again, but Trevor interrupted him once more, "What I would like to do is sell all three of you to a Muslim whorehouse where the only thing they like more than Christian virgins is an infidel who thinks their shit doesn't stink."

The captain looked up at Trevor and proclaimed, "Excuse me, but I don't know what you're talking about."

Trevor towered over the men and glanced at the guard near the door. He turned back to the three men, "I thought the purpose of vice was to stop people from committing sexual crimes, but the three of you haven't done that, have you?"

The captain regarded Trevor with apprehension, "What are you referring to?"

Trevor gave the three men a ferocious look. "How about the fact the three of you, have been sampling the forbidden fruit of those whorehouses?"

The captain stared at Trevor in fury, "You can't prove anything." Trevor picked up three folders and dropped them before the captain.

The captain investigated the first folder and handed it to the detective on his left before opening the second one. The detective on his right glanced at the pictures and grabbed the last folder. The look on his face conveyed utter despair---he didn't know Jimmy had pictures of him. The captain spoke for his team, "What are your intentions?"

Trevor pulled out the chair and sat down. He stared down the detective to the right of the captain. "Your wife is expecting, isn't she? What do you think she will do when she sees those pictures?" Trevor addressed the other detective. "And you, your fiancé has two children, a boy and a girl. What would she do?" Trevor finally addressed the captain. "You...you have three children, and your daughter is pregnant. Do any of you think that you will be allowed to see your children or grandchildren if these pictures get out? Much less, what will happen to you professionally? So, gentleman, what I'm saying is that if any of you three double-cross me; I will destroy you. Are we clear?"

The captain looked at his two detectives, "I guess we don't have much of a choice."

Trevor nodded, "No, you don't, but I need someone with your...talents. I'm setting up a charity in Athens for the girls from those houses, and I need someone to set up the security and manage it. You will, of course, behave yourselves. If I find that you're taking advantage of those girls in the slightest way, I will come down harder than you can imagine. And if you violate our agreement, the consequences will be...well, I believe I have made my point."

The captain looked at his detectives before inquiring, "What if the police get a hold of these photos?"

Trevor chuckled. "They won't."

The captain asked, "Can we talk to the Ravens?"

Trevor's expression changed to a stone-cold glare. "No!"

Trevor walked to his desk and removed a box with the two pistols. He brought them to the table and pushed them to the captain. "Here are your weapons. All the information on the Abused Women's Shelter is in that folder. Now get the hell off my property."

As they made their way out of the mansion, one guard followed them to their car. As the captain was getting in, the guard warned, "Captain, I would take heed of Mr. Paterson's words. He doesn't kid around." The captain looked at him for a second, nodded, and got into his vehicle.

Later that afternoon, after the captain had left with his detectives, Trevor went out to address the SWAT team members. They were sitting in the grass area beside their SWAT vehicle, and they had been stripped of everything: weapons, armor, and tools. They were surrounded by Trevor's security guards.

When Trevor approached the team, the leader stood up and started to yell at Trevor. Trevor just walked past him and stared down at each SWAT member. When he reached the end of the line, he turned back to the SWAT leader and interrupted him by demanding, "What's your name?"

The SWAT leader was thrown off kilter by this question. "Lieutenant Carmichael, Lt. Dave Carmichael, why?"

Trevor smiled and got right into his face. "Do you have paperwork authorizing the violation of the security of my home?"

CHAPTER 4:
The threat dealt with

The Lt was stone-faced for a moment, "No, I don't have the paperwork on me." Trevor nodded to him slowly.

"Well then...you and your men are no better than common criminals and as such, we have the right to shoot every one of you."

The SWAT team members' eyes darted up at Trevor. The Lt, who was taken aback by the statement, looked over at his men. Trevor noted the sudden realization in the Lt's face. "Now you will have a lot of questions from your superiors, so I won't keep you any longer. You can take your vehicle to return to Athens."

The Lt asked, "What about our gear?"

Trevor turned to the men, and when he heard the question, he looked back over his shoulder. "Tell your superiors that they will have to come here to retrieve them."

The Lt started to say something when Trevor interrupted him. "The right of the people to be secure in their persons, houses, papers, and effects...do you recognize those words, lieutenant? Maybe one of your men can educate you. That is the fourth amendment to the Constitution of the United States of America, and those rights can't be violated unless a warrant is issued after showing probable cause. Do you have a warrant?" The Lt's expression showed that he did not possess a warrant.

Trevor turned away and studied the expressions of the men sitting on the grass. He then turned back to the Lt. "Lieutenant, I have the feeling or at least the hope that you and your men only have the best of intentions. Today you were played by Captain Fletcher; he didn't show me any paperwork either, which means he didn't have any. He thought he could bluster his way into my home, but guess what, he was wrong. You and your men broke the law by forcing your way onto my property. I also know that you were personally informed by one of my men to not cut the fence. Do you remember what you told him?"

The LT looked at his men and then back at Trevor. He was warned, but like Captain Fletcher, he had found that he could bluster his way through. He also knew that he was in a lot of trouble for what he did.

Trevor stopped and gave him a long look then said, " I hope this will act as a learning experience, and before you do this again, you will make sure you have said documents on your person before acting. I now have a picture of every one of you, and if any of you ever attempt this again, my men will shoot to kill. Do I make myself clear?"

The Lt looked at his men and nodded his head. Sometimes those who have taken on the mantel to protect us forget that there are limitations to their power. The men began to rise and proceed to the SUV. They had to double up, to get the seven men into the SUV, but they soon left, followed by two men on a gator.

Trevor walked into his office and dialed a number in France. Maurice answered, and Trevor spoke in French. "So how much damage have they done? That is good, did they have fun? Oh really…that's terrific. I will have a jet there tomorrow morning at eight so they can return. Is that Okay…Terrific, thanks a lot, Maurice." Trevor then called Travel Jet, his private jet leasing company, and arranged for a jet to be in Paris at his chalet at eight in the morning.

The time the girls spent in Paris was like a fun-filled adventure. After Louis Vuitton, they went to David Mallett, where everyone had their hair and nails done. That afternoon at four, they went to Nina Ricci for another show, which also included some leather. Liz and Jamie enjoyed the fashions more than Susan or Samantha.

On Friday, they visited Christian Dior, where Samantha fell in love with the fashions and bought fifteen of them. Of course, the other girls also went crazy and ordered several outfits of their own. They left with over thirty outfits, which were shipped to the chalet. On Saturday evening, Maurice took them clubbing. The immigration agent and his wife joined the group, and they all danced and had a blast.

On Wednesday, just as they arrived back at the chalet, Maurice received a call from Trevor and informed the girls. They rose early and started to pack. They visited four different designers and several famous tourist attractions. Maurice ordered several sets of luggage and then had them delivered to the girls' rooms. The next morning, they required a large van to transport the luggage to the landing strip where the airplane was waiting.

At one in the afternoon, the girls arrived back in Georgia. Trevor met them on the landing strip along with a truck to haul the luggage back to the mansion. As they rode, Samantha was sitting in the passenger seat. She wore a white pantsuit with a gray silk blouse as she watched the scenery go by and listened to Jamie, Susan, and Liz in the back seat rehashing the highlights of their trip. When they exited the plane, Liz ran to Trevor and hugged him, but Samantha didn't. Instead, she gave Trevor a hard look and said, "We need to talk."

It took several trips to deliver the luggage to the two apartments. After dropping the last suitcase off in Liz's room, Trevor walked into his bedroom to find Sam hanging her last outfit in her walk-in closet. As she looked at it, she glanced at Trevor, "It still looks empty."

Trevor smiled. "Well, maybe another shopping trip is in order?"

Sam closed the door and started to walk slowly toward Trevor as her expression slowly transformed from a smile to an angry look. Trevor backed up towards the bed. He was studying her as she approached and offered, "I like that outfit on you."

Sam countered, "Yeah, it looks a lot better than your shirt, doesn't it?" When she came within arm's length, she punched him in the stomach.

Trevor huffed since he wasn't prepared, "Ouch! Why did you do that?" Sam continued to advance as he retreated. Suddenly, Trevor stepped forward, wrapped his arms around Sam's waist, picked her up, and spun around. He landed on his back on the bed with Sam on top.

Sam immediately struggled to free herself from his arms and sat up. She slapped his chest. "I'm tired of you deciding for me without even consulting me, and I want to know why we had to fly to Paris. Do you realize how embarrassing it was for Liz and me when we showed up and the only clothing, we had was what we had on? I was wearing your shirt, so all I owned were my shoes!"

Trevor chuckled as he gazed into her angry face and marveled at how beautiful she was. "All you had on was your shoes---now that I would like to see. But did you have fun?"

Sam gave him a petulant look and crossed her arms. "I decided to get even, so we spent as much of your money as we could. I hope you're sorry."

Trevor was lying on his back, grinning, and looking up at Sam. "Well since you haven't filled your closet, I don't think you spent enough."

Sam slapped him again on the chest and took in the Cheshire cat grin on his handsome face. "How much did we spend?"

"Well, so far I've only been billed for $240,000." Sam put her hands over her face in shock. Just before she left, she was upset about spending $24.00 for a dress. She looked up first then back at Trevor, but she had questions.

Sam leaned forward and rubbed her hands up the front of his shirt. "Well, if I don't get some answers, guess who is sleeping alone tonight?"

Trevor's jaw dropped. "No no no! That's cruel, honey---don't do that. How about this? If I explain what happened, will you sleep in here tonight . . . please?"

Sam gave a sly smile and relished her newly found power as she moved around on top of him. "Maybe...if I like the answer."

Trevor returned that million-dollar smile. "It's been a week. How about one kiss just to show me you liked the trip to Paris?"

Sam could feel Trevor's arousal beneath her, and a smile grew on her face as she leaned forward to place both hands beside Trevor's shoulders. She allowed the distance between their lips to shrink, "I didn't enjoy the beginning of it, but it was fun." Her lips came close to his, and when he raised his head to steal a kiss, she rose to stay out of reach. The flirtation excited her.

When Trevor dropped his head to the mattress again, she lowered her lips to his. Just as they began to touch, they heard, "Jesus Christ, we have only been home for forty-five minutes. Can't you two contain yourselves?" Both Trevor and Sam turned and locked their shared gaze to see Liz standing just inside the door to their room.

Trevor whispered, "We forgot to lock that door."

Sam looked at Trevor and scolded him. "You were the last one through that door, so you forgot."

Sam started to dismount Trevor, but he reached for her. She wiggled out of his grasp, sauntered over to Liz, and turned towards Trevor, who was still lying on the bed. Sam tapped her foot and demanded, "We are waiting."

Trevor raised his head and looked at his girls. "Give me a second...I'm not used to this." Sam and Liz giggled as they ran out of the room and slammed the door. Trevor rose from the bed and stumbled to the door. He found it locked and yelled out, "You locked me in!" He quickly unlocked the door and stepped into the living room just in time to see the elevator door close. Trevor ran to another door, flew down the steps two at a time, and exited into the foyer just as the elevator door opened.

Trevor had to catch his breath and placed both hands on each side of the elevator door. He was breathing hard while Sam and Liz studied him for a second. "He is faster than he looks," Liz teased.

Trevor looked upon them with protective adoration. "You want to know why I sent you to Paris. Follow me." He turned and headed to the control room.

Sam and Liz followed Trevor into the control room, and as Trevor entered the room, he ordered, "Gary! Bring up the pictures of the two

Athens detectives." Trevor stood between the console and the large screen. When the pictures appeared on the 60" screen, Trevor began to explain who they were. He then showed the pictures of the captain and explained what he wanted. Next, he showed the video of Jasper Grebes being lowered down by a forklift. Trevor finished with a play-by-play of how an eight-man SWAT team attempted to storm the fences only to be fended off.

Trevor then turned to Liz. "I need a favor from you."

Liz nodded. "Okay, what?"

Trevor smoothed his daughter's hair. "I have a hotel in Athens that I just finished refurbishing. It's seven floors about four or five blocks from UGA. I have also created a charity for the girls that were held in those houses, and they are being transported to the hotel, which I have also donated to the charity. Now I need the money from Jimmy Dittle's bank account transferred into an account for the charity."

Liz grinned. "No problem, Dad."

Trevor chuckled. "Now we need to go eat lunch. I'm starved."

Trevor walked over and put his arm around Sam's shoulders. She looked up at him quizzically. "What do we do now?"

Trevor looked down at her. "Well, there are several things we need to do. I need you to start going over my books and get them organized. Then I need to move you and Liz into the mansion. Most importantly, we must make arrangements for Liz's education and training."

Liz was walking with Gary out of the control room when Gary stepped up beside her and asked, "Can I look at the algorithm you used to decipher Jimmy's code?"

Liz was looking at her mother and father walking in front of them. "Sure, along with the algorithm I'm going to use on those two if they think they can decide my life for me?" Gary chuckled, and when Liz gave him an angry look, he held both hands up in surrender.

CHAPTER 5:
Settling things

Trevor, Sam, Liz, and Gary exited onto the veranda where Susan and Jamie were waiting. Jamie called out," Well it's about time!"

Liz snidely remarked, "Mom had to sit on him to get him to behave."

Susan chuckled and asked, "Oh really, what position is that called?"

Sam replied, "Woman on top." They all started to laugh.

Jamie looked at Trevor and Sam. "So, what now? Do you stay here or go back to Winder?" Sam was a cornucopia of emotions. She loved being with Trevor, but she was now thriving at work, and her reputation was earning her more exposure, which would mean more money. She was enamored by the man who swept her off her feet so many years ago, but things had changed since then. She had her own life now. Should I throw everything away I have done to come here? *Is this man committed to me?* She wasn't sure what she wanted to do or if he wanted her.

Sam looked at Jamie and replied, "I haven't decided yet."

Trevor knew Samantha had mixed emotions, but he knew what would sway her to stay. Trevor suddenly stood up and used his knife to tap on his glass and get everyone's attention.

Trevor turned to Samantha, "I have been looking for you for twelve years, and I don't want to lose you again. I want to do something I should have done fifteen years ago." Trevor dropped to one knee while pulling a ring from his pants pocket. "Samantha Raven, this is my great-grandmother's wedding ring. I am offering it to you and asking if you would honor me by being my wife. Will you marry me?"

Samantha looked up at Trevor in shock and surprise. When he spoke, her heart jumped into her throat. She had an inkling that he would propose, but she was unsure until he dropped to one knee. Her hands went to cover her mouth as she gasped at this romantic gesture. Slowly, the realization came over her that he was asking her to marry him. The man of her or any woman's dreams was asking her to take his name.

Susan looked over at Sam and asked, "Samantha so what's your answer?"

Sam's eyes filled with tears of joy as she fanned her cheeks. She turned to Liz to steady her nerves and asked, "You ready to have a father?"

Liz looked over at Trevor and smiled with a fast nod. "Sure Mom, I'm ready." Sam turned back to Trevor and tried to speak but she couldn't. She simply nodded yes, and the table erupted in cheers.

Susan asked, "So Trevor…we need your credit card again to go shopping."

"Why do you need to go shopping now?"

Jamie chimed in, "Duh! We have a wedding to shop for!"

Sam held her hands up, "Yes, yes, we do, but we need to plan first, for a lot of things. But for now, we need to eat."

The ladies sullenly sat back down, having missed another opportunity to go shopping with Trevor's money as Sam looked at Trevor, "We will have a family meeting upstairs later."

Trevor popped some food into his mouth with a smile and retorted, "No problems as long as you are in my bed tonight."

Sam gently slapped him on his arm and fired back, "You're so bad."

Trevor leaned over to whisper in her ear, "If you think I'm bad now, wait until tonight."

After dinner, Sam, Trevor, and Liz retired to their apartment to iron things out. Several issues needed immediate attention. First was merging their houses, then Elizabeth's education, and finally, their training. Trevor lived in a world where the only constant was change. It made things difficult when it came to investments.

What happened in Venezuela was a prime example. The oil companies spent billions to find and tap the large deposits of petroleum. Chavez was elected president, and he, in pure Socialist fashion, seized the most valuable assets of the country, beginning with the oil wells. All the money invested by the companies to build those wells was thrown into the wind.

For Samantha and Elizabeth to penetrate his world, they needed to learn the tricks of the trade. First, learning languages was crucial. A close second was becoming physically fit. It was necessary to ensure one had the endurance to keep up in terms of self-defense, as the last barrier when someone tried to harm the family.

For Trevor, this was a natural progression. He grew up in this world. He took his father's company far beyond his father's wildest aspirations. Samantha and Elizabeth were still green and had to accelerate their development if they just wanted to survive. This was where the decisions began.

Regarding the house in Winder, Sam didn't want to get rid of the house for many reasons. Mainly, it was the home she grew up in and a place where someone could crash if necessary. Trevor felt that Samantha should decide what was to be left in the house and what should be brought to the mansion. All their possessions and clothing would arrive, but the furniture would stay since it wasn't needed in the mansion.

Liz's education was kind of a hot-button issue because Liz liked having her summers free. Also, she wanted to see her friends from Winder High School. Trevor wanted her to take several courses over the summer and start training. All he had to do was convince Liz.

Trevor was also a jet-set businessman who had garnered enemies and friends worldwide; with Liz attending Winder High School, it presented a security gap. What if a nefarious person, kidnapped Liz from the school to be used in blackmailing Trevor? Trevor was concerned for her safety, and having a large bodyguard following her around the school wouldn't work.

Education was important to Trevor because he was home-schooled and had tutors year-round. Homeschooling can be the best or worst education. If the parents were financially able to allow one adult to remain home, the education level of the remaining parent was irrelevant because the intense attention enabled the parent to dig deeper into the subject than was normally allowed in a public or even a private school setting.

The one drawback was those subjects like math and science. If one didn't have an affinity for those subjects, then teaching them was extremely difficult. That is where the tutors came in. One tutor working with one or two students would improve the quantitative value of the instruction to the recipients and improve the education. Trevor had no problem with hiring tutors, but that meant going to school year-round. Liz wasn't too keen on this idea.

Now came the issue of training. Trevor was adamant about physical training in self-defense and keeping in shape. Every effort could be made to ensure one's safety, but in the end, an individual was always his or her last line of defense. Without these skills, bad things could always happen.

Furthermore, Sam wanted to go back to work at Hutchinson. She had worked there for six years and needed to finish the projects she had started. She also had a good friend in Jennifer Wills, and she wanted to go and at least say goodbye to her.

Not all matters had been resolved, but problems were presented, opinions were aired, and some solutions were decided. At the end of their debate, Trevor said, "Okay, I must go down to my office to send some emails. I'll be back shortly."

Once Trevor left, Sam and Liz looked at each other. Sam said, "Let's get some wine and talk."

CHAPTER 6:
Samantha and Liz finally get a chance to talk

Sam and Liz walked into the dining room in search of wine. When they found a bottle, they opened it and walked back to the living room with their glasses to sit and talk.

Liz sipped her wine and said, "These taste better than the wine we had at home."

Sam sipped hers, "Well, I was buying what was on sale." They both giggled, and Sam asked, "You said you would like to have a father, so it looks like you got your wish. How do you feel about it now?"

Liz stared at her wine glass and smiled, "I didn't expect all this additional stuff he is expecting us to do."

Sam laughed softly, "I did warn you that bringing a man into our lives would also bring changes."

Liz looked up at her mother and surmised, "I was hoping that you would have to deal with those changes, not me."

"Surprise, surprise honey! I asked, and you said you were ready. So how do we make the best of it?"

Liz took another sip and then looked away, "At least I don't have to sleep with him."

Sam chuckled and retorted, "I think that is the best part."

Liz's mood shifted as her smile faded, "Yea, but I don't think any man would want a whore as a wife."

Sam's expression changed as well, "I want to apologize for not having this talk sooner, but we have been in a whirlwind, and this is the first night where we could just sit and talk. They hurt you badly, didn't they?"

Liz replied in a near whisper, "They slapped and hit me until I complied. They made me do things I don't want to talk about." Liz looked up at her mother and asked, "I heard that Jamie and Susan rescued you from Roger Dawson. What happened?"

Sam took a sip from her wine glass and thought about how much she should say. She realized that they both were forced to do abhorrent things, so she decided that this time, it would be wise for Liz to know what happened.

Sam lowered her glass and made eye contact with her daughter as she clasped their hands together, "One week before you were kidnapped, they found secure documents in my car. They were going to charge me with corporate espionage and put me in jail for ten years. You would have gone into child protective services and become a ward of the state. I couldn't allow that to happen."

Liz's eyes grew larger, "What did you have to do?"

Sam kept her stone face and slowly replied, "I had to meet with Roger Dawson two times a week for what he called 'consultations,' but actually, it was so he could . . . rape me." Liz put her hand to her mouth, then looked down and she suddenly realized that she wasn't alone in this treacherous experience.

Sam continued with her hands firmly gripped on her daughter's fragile fingers. "What I had to endure was nothing like what you went through, but the bottom line here is that neither you nor I did anything wrong, I was fighting to keep you safe; you were fighting to stay alive. But we did nothing wrong. I'm not going to allow Roger to define me, and you can't allow a bottom feeder like Jimmy Dittle to define you."

Liz thought for a minute. "When I was researching Jimmy Dittle, I found Roger Dawson who was his friend in high school. They had a reputation for raping girls and forcing them into prostitution."

Sam sat back in shock. "Well, let's hope this chapter is over---we need to close it."

Tears streamed down Liz's cheeks in torrents. "How do I do that?"

Sam took Liz's wine glass and placed both of their glasses on the coffee table before them. She reached over and dragged Liz into her lap as she so often did when Liz was a child. She wrapped her arms around her. Liz protested, "What are you doing? I'm not a baby anymore."

"I'm your mother, and I want to hold you---now come here."

Liz rolled her eyes. "Oh geez, mom!"

Liz relented and moved closer with her legs across Sam's legs as Sam embraced her. Sam then said, "You decide who you are. You wanted to go back to school, and I will do whatever I can to accomplish that. But you know there are a lot of small-minded people at that school, and they will take this opportunity to belittle you. Take the training that Trevor is offering and defend yourself. You just accomplished what most of those girls couldn't handle, but you prevailed. Don't ever take any shit from anyone."

Liz was crying more now. "So, I can kick some ass if I want to?"

Sam held her harder. "Just make sure it's justified. If you start wailing on one of those skinny little cheerleaders, it will be hard to defend you."

Liz started to giggle then Sam began giggling. They both burst into laughter as they sat back and looked at each other. Liz asked, "What about sex? If that was sex, I never want to experience it again. I thought Dad was torturing you that day. Susan had to sit me down to keep me from coming to your aid."

Sam smiled, "Honey, what you experienced was rape---that is not sex. That is someone imposing their will over you. What Trevor was doing to me was . . . Oh God, it was glorious and fantastic. I've been dreaming of what he did to me, and I can't wait for him to do it again. That is the difference. Sex between two consenting people who love each other is not rape. It cements their souls. You strip yourself bare, expose yourself, and hide nothing from each other. That is what makes the marriage work."

"So, you're saying I should listen to Dad and at least try?"

Sam nodded, "You need to go to the gym and work out, but on the upside, Jamie and Susan will teach you how to defend yourself. So, what if you must take a few courses during the summer? Negotiate---you don't have to accept everything he wants. And you know damn well that your father is in the palm of your hand. He adores you."

Sam reached over and retrieved both glasses of wine. She handed Liz hers back as they separated a little, "Much of what he is requesting is for our safety---his world is significantly more dangerous than our world, but here we are."

Liz responded with a smirk, "Yeah, and look what happened to both of us."

Sam chuckled and tilted her head, "So, what is it you don't like most of his suggestions?"

Liz stared at the fireplace as she sipped her wine, "The gym---you know I have never been big on Phys Ed. I don't know if I can do all that physical stuff."

Sam nodded and asked, "What about the driving?"

"I can already drive, but I'm not sure what kind of driving he is talking about."

"I'm not sure either, but remember what Jamie and Susan did--- would you like to be able to do that?" Liz took another sip of her wine and remained silent while she pondered the question.

"I don't know if I could ever be as bad as those two women. They were awesome--- I couldn't believe what I was seeing! I think I would like to learn what they know."

Sam nodded, "When I arrived here, Jamie escorted me around and she said that they spend most of the day in the gym training. You remember me telling you of watching Trevor in the ring against

Susan?" Liz nodded, and Sam continued, "They work diligently to stay on top of their game, which means they have to work out every day."

Suddenly, the door to the elevator opened. Trevor stepped out and stopped as he looked at both women. Trevor saw that Sam and Liz were sitting closely on the couch with glasses of wine and talking. He didn't know exactly what they were talking about, but there was a good chance that he was the subject of the conversation. He decided that he didn't want to interrupt their discussion, so he pointed to his bedroom door and quickly disappeared through it.

Liz was looking over her shoulder at the bedroom door, "Will I have to put up with you screaming tonight?"

Sam gave her a gentle slap on her knee, "I wasn't screaming."

Liz took a sip of her wine as she looked intently at her mother, the two were only a foot apart now, and Sam replied, "Okay, maybe a little, but I will be quieter tonight. You won't hear a peep."

Liz smiled playfully, "How long are you going to keep him waiting?"

Sam smiled then killed her wine and handed the wine glass to Liz, "I will work on him tonight, but I want you to consider what he was saying. We are entering his world, and he knows what he's dealing with." Liz took the glass and nodded. Both women rose. Liz headed to the kitchen and Sam through the bedroom door.

As Sam entered the master bedroom, she used her back to gently push the door closed and lock it. She watched as Trevor exited the bathroom wearing only pajama bottoms. He looked delicious with his six-pack abs and hard physique as he stopped in mid-step to admire Sam.

Sam walked slowly to the far side of the bed, and with a wicked smile, Trevor ambled to the opposite side. Trevor began circling the bed towards Sam, but she climbed onto the mattress. When Trevor reached her side, she spun across the bed and trotted to the bathroom door. She turned to look at Trevor, who was in shock as he watched her shoot him a mischievous smile before backing into the bathroom and closing the door.

Trevor trotted to the door, checked it, and found it locked. He tapped on the door. "Is everything okay, honey?" Sam was undressing and replied, "I'm fine---I will be out in a minute" With a shit-eating grin on his face, Trevor retreated towards the bed and lowered the lights. He looked around the room and decided that she would want the side closest to the bathroom, so he pulled the duvet off and then lost his pajama bottoms before jumping into the bed and sliding to the middle. He covered himself with the sheet as he lay on his side, eagerly watching the door to the bathroom.

CHAPTER 7:
Sam Hears Trevor's Side of the Story

Finally, after several excruciating minutes, the door unlocked, and Samantha appeared wearing his robe. She saw him waiting in the bed and took her time approaching it. She could sense his impatience, and he was doing everything he could to not jump out of the bed and grab her. When she reached her side of the bed, she slowly untied the robe and opened it, allowing it to fall to the floor---she was wearing nothing. Sam slowly crawled into the bed and slid over next to him. Trevor leaned in to kiss her when she put her fingers between their lips and said, "We need to talk first."

Trevor nodded slowly and whispered, "Okay."

Sam slid her hands under the covers, and as she suspected, he was naked as well. She gently ran her hands down his side and across his pelvic region. She wrapped her fingers around his already erect penis and cooed; "Now I will know if you lie to me."

Trevor gave a pained smile and replied in a voice one octave higher, "Okay, honey."

Sam moved closer while keeping a firm hold on Trevor's lower brain. "I still remember the last time we spent the night together."

Trevor gave a wry smile, "I have replayed that night in my head so many times." Sam moved her hand up and down a little while Trevor moved up and looked down into Sam's face. Those lips, those eyes---he longed to kiss her.

Sam asked, "That day at the bus station---what happened?"

With an anxious look on his face, Trevor explained, "The director of security at that time called to inform me that my parents had been murdered in Pakistan, and they needed me home immediately."

Sam stopped moving her hand. She understood the aspects of losing her parents. She had lost hers, but they weren't murdered. She nodded sympathetically, "What did you do?"

Trevor moved his hand to her side and pulled her closer. "I went home, of course, and then flew to Islamabad."

"To get the bodies?"

"At first, yes. I worked for the Peace Corps for two years in Gujranwala, Pakistan, which is where they make most of the hand-carved rosewood furniture sold there. During those two years, I became fluent in Urdu, their native language. I contacted a friend, an AROS, at the embassy and learned that the Islamabad police wouldn't investigate because it happened in Rawalpindi. In Rawalpindi, they don't consider killing an infidel a crime. I realized that if I wanted justice for my parents, I had to do it myself."

Sam wasn't moving now as she investigated Trevor's face and could only imagine the pain he felt. "What did you do?"

Trevor moved some hair behind her ear, "If you remember, I had long hair and a beard. I was also fluent in their language; I put on their clothes and began hunting them down. I found the three men and took my revenge, I then hunted down the bastard who ordered the hit and gave him exactly what he deserved. Please don't ask what I did because I wasn't kind or merciful. I respect the Pakistani people because they are good, hardworking honest people---but the Taliban are thugs. They don't respect kindness, only strength. In their world, women are to be possessed, and only Muslim men are of any value.

Trevor took a breath and continued, "They don't like entrepreneurs; they consider businessmen unworthy. In Islam, a strong man walks in and takes what he wants. They despised my parents because they, among other things, were businesspeople. They had invested thirty million dollars into a glass factory in Rawalpindi that employed almost a thousand people. After my parents were murdered, the director of

Pakistan Gas in Islamabad informed the CEO of the glass factory that if they wanted any natural gas, they had to pay a higher bribe to him. They couldn't afford it, so he cut off the gas, which closed the factory."

Trevor sighed as he shared one of his most traumatic memories. "Islam is like socialism in the sense that those in power want the people to be dependent on them, not on themselves. So, when I arrived, I began my search. I had to travel from Karachi to Peshawar to find them, and I found each one. I killed them and anyone who defended them. My parents were not political. They believed in capitalism because it creates jobs, and jobs help the people." Trevor was looking intently into Sam's face and saw the tear that rolled down her cheek. He wiped it with his thumb.

Sam whispered, "I'm sorry."

Trevor didn't smile but spoke softly, "No, it is I who should apologize. I fled to India in a small boat to escape the authorities who wanted to kill me. When I returned, I learned that you had been looking for me because you were pregnant with my child. My security and CFO were both furious. They explained to me that I took unreasonable risks to exact my revenge. What I should have done was hire some people to find them and deliver them to me. I selfishly put myself at risk, as well as my company. I also missed seeing my daughter's birth and childhood, which is a real loss that I can't repay. It took me three years to exact my revenge. Even when I finished, it still hurt. The pain of their loss still haunts me."

Trevor released a sigh and continued, "I have been looking for you for twelve years. I thought I had found you several times only to get there too late. It was frustrating. Morgenstern mentioned a Samantha Raven in this area doing wonderful things, but it wasn't until I talked to Steve Bushier, who told me how to find you. I wasn't sure until you walked in that day. That was why I drove to your house and infuriated you. I'm sorry for doing that, but I wanted to see my daughter, and I wanted to see you again. You're still as beautiful as ever, and I can't believe I have you here."

Sam was mesmerized by the story and had a hard time holding back tears. She pushed Trevor onto his back and kissed him. She then followed those kisses down his chest and began to make love to her man as only an enamored woman could. For the second time in a week, she gave herself to Trevor and showered him with her love. An hour later, they fell asleep in each other's arms.

Several hours later, Trevor moved first and realized that the dream was real. Samantha Raven was asleep in his arms. Trevor checked the clock, and it was only 5 in the morning. He lifted her and moved her to the center of the bed before he began touching and caressing her. As he gradually aroused her, she moved and moaned but didn't wake. Trevor's desire and passionate demeanor intensified as he mounted her in the missionary position and entered her.

He began a slow and methodical undulation inside of her. Sam was still dreaming, and Trevor admired her face, the arch of her back, and her slightly open mouth. He savored the visual indications of her orgasm. He continued his blissful torture, and Sam raised her legs to his sides. As she came into a second orgasm, she opened her eyes to find him on top of her as she stared straight into his soul. She screamed in ecstasy, "It is you, oh God! It's you."

Trevor continued rutting her gently, and she gripped onto him as her third orgasm consumed her. He held her stare, "What are you doing to me? Oh, dear God!"

"I'm making love to you again. Remember what we did last night?" Trevor could read her thoughts through her smile, and he quickened his rhythm. A girlish squeal escaped from Sam as she had another orgasm. He smiled in satisfaction, "It makes me happy that just the thought of what I did to you last night gives you an orgasm."

Sam kissed him again, "You are so bad." Trevor sped up the pace as he plunged into her depths, and she held onto him as he delivered her into her final orgasm. She squealed so loudly that she startled herself and quickly covered her mouth.

Trevor chuckled and asked, "Why did you do that?" Sam gave him a shy look. "I promised Liz, she wouldn't hear me scream." Trevor began to laugh, and Sam had to give him a gentle slap. "Naughty boy!

What time is it?" Trevor leaned in, kissed her, and said, "It's five thirty." Sam looked up at him in shock. "You woke me up at five thirty?"

Trevor gave her a big smile and replied, "Because we need to be in the gym at six."

Sam pushed the hair out of her face. "So, you woke me up this early so we can go to the gym?"

"No, I woke you up this early so I could watch you having orgasms in your sleep."

Sam tried to feign shock but instead let a small smile escape from her mouth, pushing him gently on his chest, "Yeah, you are bad. What have I gotten myself into?"

Trevor started to laugh and jumped out of bed, "I suggest we take a quick shower so that when we start to sweat, we won't smell like sex."

Sam's eyes lingered on him as he exited the bed. She lay there for a second thinking of what he had just done to her and shook her head as she rolled out of bed. She suddenly realized that last night had left her sore, but she smiled anyway.

As she headed to the bathroom, she thought, the best way to get rid of the soreness was to do it again.

CHAPTER 8:
Striking a Deal with Mat

They hit the gym, and later that morning, they went to the house in Winder to pack it up. Trevor spotted the shy Mathew Chambers. Trevor pulled Sam to the side and asked, "What's the story with the young boy?" They were inside the house, and Sam was directing the movers.

She peered out the front window at Matt sitting on the front porch with Liz beside him. "The day we moved in, he came over and helped. He was only seven, but he desperately wanted to help. He and Liz have known each other ever since. Why do you ask?"

"He might be the answer to Liz's bodyguard problem at school."

Trevor grabbed a box, headed to the truck, and walked back to the front porch to introduce himself then asked, "You're Mathew, right?" Matt looked at Liz and then back at Trevor. He nodded nervously.

Trevor smiled and said, "Take a walk with me." Matt looked at Trevor with utter disdain. Trevor was the man taking his best friend away, so he didn't like him.

Matt glanced at Liz as she pushed him with her elbow and urged," Go ahead." Matt got up and walked into the front yard with Trevor as they talked, they soon meandered over to Mathew's house next door. Trevor asked questions of Matt about what he wanted in the future, his likes, his dislikes, etc.

Mathew's father was in the driveway working on their old car when Trevor and Matt wandered over. Matt proudly announced, "My dad can fix just about anything." Mr. Chambers appeared from under the hood wiping his hands with a rag and nodded to Trevor. Mr. Chambers was over six feet tall and a little round around in the middle with thick arms from hard work. He offered a fist bump since his hands were covered in oil and grease.

Mathew made the introductions. "Dad, this is Trevor Paterson. This is my dad, Nat Chambers."

Trevor asked, "So what's wrong with it?"

Nat replied, "Oil job. I like changing my oil."

Trevor nodded and asked, "K&W filters?"

Nat nodded his head. "Not for the oil, but the air cleaner is."

Trevor rubbed his chin. "I do that for my truck, but I don't have the time to do it myself. I like the K&W air filters. They breathe better than the paper filters."

"Is that your green truck out there?"

"Yes sir."

Matt watched for several minutes as the two men discussed engine sizes and accessories. It was male bonding at its best. He knew Trevor was rich, but he learned that Trevor didn't like wasting money when he didn't need to. Trevor saw a swinging bench on the porch of Matt's house and asked, "Sir I'd like to speak with your son for a minute. Is that okay?" Mr. Chambers looked at his son, who nodded. Trevor shook Nat's hand and guided Matt away. "Matt, let's go up here and talk."

They walked to the front porch of Matt's house and sat on the bench. Matt seemed to read Trevor's mind, "I could watch over her, sir." Trevor darted his eyes to Matt and nodded with a smile. When Matt was talking to Liz, she mentioned Trevor's concern about her safety. Trevor could tell that this boy was sharp-minded.

Trevor had taken the time to walk to Matt's house and talk to his dad to size up Matt, who was five foot eleven and a pudgy one hundred and eighty pounds. His father was much taller and stronger. After meeting, his father he realized that he came from good stock and that his father was a levelheaded, down-to-earth type of man. This background impressed Trevor. He crossed his arms as he watched Matt's father working and asked, "You think you're bad enough to defend her?"

Matt sat up straight and replied with confidence, "I will begin working out every day, sir, and I will be ready in the fall."

Trevor grinned. He liked this boy, "Matt, I don't doubt your dedication but what I want to know is: how far are you willing to go to protect her?"

Matt looked at Trevor for a second then replied, "Sir, she doesn't know it, but I love her. I will give my life for her."

Trevor's grin grew larger, "I believe that son, but what I'm looking for is someone willing to come to my home and work with my people on getting into shape and learning self-defense. It will require at least four hours every day in the gym in addition to working on the plantation. It takes a lot of work to keep it running."

Matt sat up, "I will do it, sir."

Trevor chuckled and looked at him for a few seconds, "You have a driver's license?"

Matt was sitting up straight, trying to show Trevor how tough he was, "Yes sir, but I don't have a car yet."

"Okay, come with me." They walked over to Trevor's truck. Trevor reached inside, grabbed his GPS, and handed it to Mathew.

Trevor instructed, "Tomorrow is Saturday. Have your mother drop you off at six. Just hit home and it will guide you. When you get there, I will have my people look you over, now the only thing we need to discuss is: what are you worth per hour?"

Negotiating a salary was an area in which Matt had little experience. Other than working around his house, he had yet to find a job.

However, he felt that he could negotiate something. "Twenty an hour, sir. After all, this is for Liz."

Trevor smiled at Matt's attempt to negotiate with him. It was obvious that Trevor was worried about his daughter, so Mathew was trying to use Trevor's love for Elizabeth to negotiate a higher salary. This impressed Trevor. Trevor replied, "I was thinking ten an hour, and you're right. This is for Liz, the girl you love." Trevor knew Mathew loved Elizabeth, so he was using Mathew's love for her as leverage.

Matt nodded and was quiet for a second as he thought about the offer, "What about fifteen, sir? Because this is for Liz, and I'm going to do whatever is necessary to protect her."

Trevor gave him a big smile, and with a chuckle, he shook Matt's hand, "Deal."

Trevor looked over at Sam and Liz directing the traffic of the movers, "Matt, I have one more problem that you can hopefully help me with."

Matt had a big grin on his face. He now liked Trevor for giving him a job, especially one that would require him to hang out with Elizabeth, "Name it, sir."

Trevor turned away from the house, placing his foot onto the running board of the old, green Ford truck. He used his left hand to rub his lower lip and asked, "When Sam called the school Thursday and asked to bring Liz back to school, the principal refused to allow her back in. He told Sam that since she missed the exams, she would have to repeat the year."

Matt nodded and turned to look at the women. With his right foot propped on the same running board, he replied, "Yeah, he is kind of anal, but they are trying to raise money for new uniforms for the band and football team. You might be able to work a deal there."

Trevor leaned in closer to Mathew, "This bodyguard thing . . . that is our secret, okay?"

Matt smiled, "For Liz." Trevor shook Matt's hand again and returned to the house as Sam and Liz watched him.

Sam was leaving all the furniture and kitchen items, but she wanted most of her clothes and that picture hidden in the drawer of her bedside table. The truck wasn't full, but they had what they wanted. After locking the door to the house, they headed back to the Plantation. Matt walked over to Liz and helped her carry the last box to the truck.

Liz looked over at Trevor talking to Sam. She turned to Matt, "So…what did he say? Leave my daughter alone?!"

Matt laughed. "No, he just talked to my father and then offered me a job at his house."

Liz's eyes widened, "He did?" Her expression took on a contemplative tone, "Why did he do that?"

"I don't know. I thought I was never going to see you again, but now it looks like I will be able to see you every day."

Liz looked back at her new father, "I wonder what he is up to."

Matt chuckled. He knew Liz like the back of his hand, "I thought you liked him?"

Liz looked back at Matt, "I do, but he is always up to something. Did you know he put cameras in our house, tapped our phone, and put a GPS on Mom? You must watch him."

"Well, I'm just glad that I can still come see you every day."

Liz smirked, "I hope he is paying you. He can afford it. What is your job?"

Matt shrugged his shoulders, "Not sure really. He said I need to go the gym, and he wants his people to evaluate me."

Liz wrinkled her nose at this suggestion, "Yeah, he is hung up on working out and self-defense. He told Mom and me that we must be in the gym every day as well."

"So…I get to see you sweat?"

Liz blushed and gave him a sly smile, "Correction. We get to see each other sweat."

Matt wondered about Susan and Jamie, "Those two women who came over that day---will they be at this Plantation?"

"They are his bodyguards, and I'll bet they will be instrumental in our training."

Matt's expression changed to one of intimidation, "Oh shit! I didn't think about that! That tall, blonde chick scares the hell out of me."

CHAPTER 9:
Working things out at the Plantation

Back at the Plantation, Liz had to pick her bedroom and was now discussing her education and training. Trevor was home-schooled as a child, so he was accustomed to year-round school. He received a rigorous education, and by the time he reached seventeen, he had achieved the equivalent of a two-year college education. He was fluent in French and Spanish, and he passed the college tests in mathematics, science, and history with flying colors. Trevor wanted Liz to experience this type of education.

In the apartment at the mansion, Sam and Elizabeth placed their clothes and personal items into their rooms before meeting Trevor in the living room. As they took a seat on the sofa, Trevor stood beside the fireplace and explained, "I grew up with this schedule, but I do understand your aversion to it."

Liz frowned, "Why do I have to be in the gym so early?"

Trevor retorted, "Well, your mother and I will be there as well."

Sam spoke up, "Excuse me, but why are you dragging me into this?"

Trevor chortled, "What time did you normally leave to go to work? You don't have that long drive anymore, so why not spend the extra time in the gym?"

Liz looked at her mother and mocked her, "Ha, ha!"

With a sullen face, Sam glanced at her daughter, "Shut up." Trevor and Liz burst into laughter while Sam stuck her tongue out at both.

Trevor continued, "Well, Matt will be here by six and he will spend at least two hours in the gym every morning then two more in the afternoon."

Liz perked up, "Okay, well maybe I can make it in the morning."

Trevor gave his daughter a thumbs up, "We need to discuss what subjects you should study this summer."

Liz's disgust with her father was written all over her face, "You said something about driving."

"Yes, we do a lot of driver training here."

Liz glanced frantically at her mother and back at Trevor. Trevor asked, "Do you know how to drive?"

Liz stuck her chin in the air, "I can drive an automatic, why?"

Trevor smiled, "That's good, but you won't be learning how to drive an automatic."

Liz looked at her mother and back at Trevor again, "Why not?"

"Because if you can drive a stick shift, you can drive anything."

Liz eyed Trevor suspiciously, "When can we start driving?"

Trevor gave her a grin, "That depends on if you're willing to take three classes this summer."

"Three?! Do I have to take three classes? How about one, I can take one class."

Trevor glanced at Sam then with a slight smile, "Well, I understand that this is new to you, but what would you say to two classes?"

Liz looked over at her mother, who just raised her eyebrows to look at Liz but didn't say a word. Liz looked back at Trevor, "What classes?"

Trevor knew he had her convinced, "I was thinking of getting Gary to instruct you in computer technology and Spanish, how's that?"

Liz was shocked at the class choice. She was fascinated with computers, but Spanish didn't interest her, "Spanish?! Why Spanish?"

"Well, I figured I have several people on the Plantation who already speak Spanish, and since we are getting married soon, we can take our honeymoon in Spain. I have an olive plantation there."

Liz's and Sam's eyes went wide at this revelation. Liz asked, "Can Matt come with us?"

Sam spoke up, asking indignantly, "Aren't you afraid of him hearing me scream?"

Liz leered at her mother and snidely remarked, "Well, I only heard a couple of peeps this morning, so I think you're getting a handle on him." Sam gave her a wide-eyed, open-mouthed look and tossed the pillow at Liz, "What are you doing, listening at the door?"

Liz chuckled and retorted, "Not really, but I knew I was right when you got upset. You told on yourself." Sam huffed and looked away.

Trevor chuckled at the banter between his girls, "Okay, tomorrow is Saturday, and Matt will arrive here at six for his evaluation before Jamie and Susan begin training him. After you spend two hours in the gym and agree to two classes, we will have breakfast before we go driving." Liz's eyes grew larger than ever as she looked at her mother in shock.

Liz liked Trevor but didn't want him ruling over her and dictating what she did. However, she realized that there was a give and take, and she was doing what he wanted and getting what she wanted. Trevor rose and as he headed towards the elevator, "Okay, I need to prepare for tomorrow."

Sam and Liz looked at each other for several seconds. Sam walked into the kitchen and returned with two glasses of wine. Liz gladly accepted the wine glass, "I'm not sure about your boyfriend."

Sam gave a chuckle and asked, "You mean your father, but please, explain."

"I feel like he is very controlling, and he wants me to do things I don't want to do."

Sam nodded, "So, you don't want to get up early and go to the gym; you don't want to take courses over the summer; and what was the other thing you don't want?"

Liz's expression gave a defiant expression, "I forgot." Sam chuckled.

Liz took a sip of wine, "He hired Matt to work here. What is that about?"

"So, you don't want to study computers or learn Spanish before we go to Spain, and you don't want him to teach you to drive. I'm not sure about Matt---maybe he saw how forlorn the two of you looked, or maybe he thought bringing him here would make you happy."

Liz pondered these possibilities, "No . . . I'm not sure, but there are a lot of changes, and I'm not sure. I was looking forward to spending the summer with Matt and my friends and taking it easy."

Sam took a sip, "Let me get this straight. Instead of studying computers, and Trevor has some nice computers, and learning Spanish before we go to Spain, you want to be lazy?" Liz gave Sam a disgruntled look and gulped her wine. She pretended to be enthralled by the fireplace before looking back at her mother, who had one eyebrow raised as if she were waiting for an answer to her rhetorical question. Finally, Sam smiled and broke the silence. "I know change can be hard, and this is the first time in your young life that you must deal with a massive change. But what Trevor is offering, I think, is worth the extra work he is asking us to do."

Liz stared at her mother. "Wait a minute. You're telling me that you don't mind getting up at six to hit the gym or do the other stuff he is demanding?"

"First off, he is waking me up earlier than that, and let's face it, we both could use some exercise. I need to get into shape for no other reason than to keep up with him."

Liz's eyes grew large as she snidely retorted, "Wait . . . that was you when I heard those yelps at five a.m.?" Sam remained tight-lipped with a pensive smile. Liz teased her. "What can't handle him, mom?"

Sam took a drink of her wine and pointed a finger at her daughter, "That young woman is none of your business, but I haven't been with a man for fifteen years, and he happens to be in really good shape." Sam pulled her legs onto the couch and clutched her knees. "Let's just leave it at the fact that we both need to get in shape."

Liz smiled, watching her mother wither at the thought of Trevor making love to her, "So that was you."

"You need to stop listening at our door." Liz giggled again.

Sam felt a little buzzed from the wine, "Look! I didn't know he was going to wake me up like that."

Liz held her head back and laughed, "Aha! He wakes you up in the middle of the night. Yeah! I see why you need to get into shape."

Sam rolled her eyes and took another sip of wine, "He was intolerable as a young man, but now, he is so much more. I'm finding it intimidating trying to catch up."

"That is what he said about you."

Sam almost spit her red wine all over the sofa, "He told you that? When did he say that?"

Liz delayed her response by taking a drink of her wine and finally said, "That day he convinced me to come here, I asked him what he thought of you. He said that you were impressive as a young woman, but now you are so much more." Sam's eyes grew larger as she sat back a little and smiled. At that moment, the elevator doors opened. Trevor stepped out and saw the two women on the couch, each with a glass of wine. He smiled lovingly and continued to the master bedroom.

Liz and Sam watched him over the back of the sofa as he disappeared then looked at each other and laughed, "You better hope your man isn't one of those never tiring, always moving, with endless stamina types," Sam whispered cautiously to her daughter.

This time, Liz almost choked on her wine. "Ha! What makes you think I wouldn't want that kind of man?"

Sam leaned forward and whispered, "Because you're supposed to go to bed to rest."

They both started to giggle. Sam looked over her shoulder to the door of the master bedroom where her future husband was going to bed. Liz eyed her knowingly, "Just can't wait, huh?"

Sam rolled her eyes in annoyance, "That's not it. I have always dreamed of having a man to sleep with . . . "Liz interrupted by saying, "But apparently, he doesn't sleep."

Sam giggled and shook her finger at her daughter, "When we were dating, I always felt that I was just a one-year fling, and he would be a jet-set businessman flying around in private jets with supermodels. I never dreamed that he wanted more than that."

"What about when he dropped to one knee and proposed?"

Sam could not hold back her smile as she cherished that moment, "I still wasn't sure. I knew he liked me, but I thought it was you, his daughter; he wanted you in his life. Now I'm in awe that he's been searching for me for so long."

Liz held out her hand to Sam, who looked at her daughter with the love that only a mother has for a child. She finished her glass of wine, handed it to her daughter, and stood up. "I promise I won't be screaming tonight."

Liz snorted, "Ha! Well, don't worry about it, Mom, because you haven't been able to keep quiet one night yet. If I hear a yelp, I will just assume it's business as usual."

Sam shot Liz a light-hearted yet dour look and wagged her finger at her charmingly precocious daughter before she slipped into the bedroom for the evening.

CHAPTER 10:
Setting the schedule

Saturday morning came early and on schedule, as it always does. It was five in the morning when Trevor woke and felt Sam lying next to him, naked again, despite coming to bed in a nightgown. Trevor hadn't planned to do anything but after looking at her for several seconds, he couldn't resist touching her and exploring her body as he had the morning before.

Soon enough, Sam was moaning again in her dreamlike state, and Trevor slid over to begin their morning ritual. Sam instinctually reached up and held onto his shoulder as Trevor began filling her and began a slow gentle stroke, driving into her. She opened her eyes and smiled up into Trevor's face, "I do like being awakened like this."

Trevor drank Sam in with his eyes, "So, what were you dreaming about?" Sam giggled. "It was a strange dream. I don't know if I should talk about it." Trevor hadn't stopped working her and asked, "Go ahead, it's only us here." Sam gave him a coy look, "I was talking to my mother, and she asked me what I was doing, I told her I was having sex with you, and she told me to wake up and tell you thank you." Trevor smirked, "Well you just tell your mother thank you for raising a daughter that I like waking this way." Sam beamed with delight, "Okay."

After ten minutes of sex, Trevor went into the bathroom to take a shower. Sam rolled out of bed then crept into the bathroom and opened the shower door curtain. "Got room for me?" Trevor's face revealed a devilish grin, "Only if you let me wash you." The shower took twice as long.

At six a.m., Trevor dragged Sam into the gym, but she had a gigantic smile on her face. Trevor dropped Sam with Jamie and Susan and began his routine on the elliptical. Jamie asked Susan "Is that one of those morning-delight smiles?"

Susan looked intently at Sam. "It is, it is, she got a special morning delight."

Sam suddenly realized what they were saying, so she stood up straight to hide her embarrassment, "I have no idea what you're referring to."

Jamie rubbed Sam's shoulders affectionately, "Well I think that is great---he pumped you full of endorphins, so you won't feel the pain we intend to heap upon you." Sam's mouth dropped open in shock.

Bleary-eyed and groggy, Liz wandered into the gym, "I thought I heard you two this morning."

Susan extended her hand to Liz, "Come with me little one, so I can get you started."

Jamie turned to Sam, "This will be fun."

At that moment, an old Buick exited the forest outside and slammed on the brakes when the mansion came into view. It started again and slowly proceeded to the front door. Susan's phone buzzed, signaling Matt's arrival. Susan watched Liz on the treadmill, trotting along at 2 mph, "You still have more minutes. No stopping." Liz smiled and gave her a salute.

Matt's mother slowed down in front of the mansion as they looked around when Susan suddenly walked out of the front door and opened the car door, "Come on young man, we have been waiting." She looked into the car and winked at his mother, "We will bring him home."

His mother smiled and yelled to her son, "Have fun!"

Matt stood looking at Susan, whose stance resembled that of a drill sergeant this morning. She commanded, "Come on boy. I've been looking forward to this."

Matt looked at his mother driving away, sighed, and mumbled," God help me."

When Liz saw him enter the gym, she was struggling and sweating but waved and started to dismount. She was hoping that this was a good excuse to cut her time short on the treadmill, but Susan yelled out, "Don't you dare! If you get off, the time starts over." Liz got back on and continued to jog with a frown. Matt gave a low wave to Liz and smiled, but he didn't move towards her.

Susan walked to a table along the wall and motioned for him to get onto the scales. Another man came over and recorded his weight and height. He also used a device that pinched his belly and measured his fat-to-muscle ratio. The man then took his heart rate, blood pressure, and a blood sample. Finally, he placed a wristwatch on Mathew and guided him to Susan, who was standing beside a treadmill at the end of the line six machines away from Liz.

Matt walked to Susan and glanced back at the man behind him. She motioned for him to mount the treadmill. Once he did, she started the machine at a slow pace and asked, "So Matt, did you eat breakfast this morning?"

Matt gave her a quizzical look, "Yeah, I had cereal. My mother wouldn't let me leave if I didn't . . ."

"From now on, don't eat before coming here. We eat after we work out."

Matt had questions, "Who was that man, and what was all the stuff?"

"That is our nutritionist, and he will start setting up a diet for you."

"I don't understand?"

Susan smiled and explained, "Mathew, you are at the age when either you or your body decides your physique. If you do nothing, you will grow up fat and sloppy, but we are going to put your body under stress. We are going to work you hard. It will hurt, and you will sweat, but when we are finished, you will be a new and improved man."

Liz finished her stint and walked towards Susan and Matt. Susan turned to her, "Where do you think you're going? No, you don't have time to talk. Come with me." Susan walked her over to the nutritionist, who began taking the same measurements. Once she was finished, Susan set her up on another Nautilus machine. Susan instructed, "You got fifteen minutes." Meanwhile, Jamie checked Samantha's treadmill routine.

Samantha looked at Jamie, "Do you do this with everyone?"

"Yes, he just got here, which was why Matt was first. But as soon as you're finished, I'm taking you to him."

Sam looked over at the man, "Is that all he does?"

"He is on contract with Trevor, and he monitors all of us to keep us in top physical health." Sam watched several more people arrive at the gym and go through the same process before beginning their workouts.

Matt jogged along easily until the treadmill sped up to one and a half mph...two, then finally to three. He didn't want Susan to know that he was struggling, but she could see it. She reached up and tapped on the wristwatch, which displayed his heart rate and blood pressure, and recorded it on a clipboard. When she hit the stop button, she motioned for him to follow her over to the barbells and have a seat on the bench.

Susan handed him a ten-pound barbell and told him to start doing curls. She sat across from him and mirrored him with a twenty-pound barbell. Matt reached thirty reps before she stopped him and replaced it with a twenty-pounder. Susan grabbed a thirty to keep a synchronized pace with him. Matt returned the twenty and picked up a thirty, but Matt was struggling to keep up with Susan, who was now curling with forty pounds. Regardless, Matt was determined to keep up. Jamie returned from dropping Sam off with the nutritionist and asked, "Matt, you think you can keep up with her?"

Matt did not want to be outdone by a woman, "Yeah!"

Susan grinned, returned the forty, and picked up the fifty with the same arm as she continued without skipping a beat. Matt got ahead of himself and grabbed the fifty, but he could barely complete a single rep. Jamie offered some wisdom, "You do realize she does three sets of fifty reps with a sixty-pound barbell, right?"

Matt dropped the barbell, collapsed against the back of the bench, and stared in awe at both women, "Look, if you intended to make me look bad, you succeeded."

Susan stopped and chuckled then leaned in closer to him, speaking softly, "No, what I want you to understand is that I'm your goal. By the end of this summer, I expect you to not only keep pace with me but surpass me. I know why you're here, and don't think for one second that we aren't going to push you as hard as possible to make sure you can handle the job."

Matt sat back in shock, then glanced over at Liz, then looked back at Susan and Jamie, "You won't hear me complain again."

They spent two hours that morning deciding Matt's fitness level before mapping out a customized regime. Afterward, the group enjoyed a hearty breakfast together before Liz joined Trevor for driver training. Meanwhile, the director of security whisked Matt away for a tour of the fence. Matt moved slower than usual because he ached in areas of his body that he didn't even know had significant amounts of muscle. Jeff found his awkward and disjointed movements highly amusing. Matt gave him a quizzical look, "Does everyone get this treatment?"

Jeff doubled over in laughter, "Only those in security." They cruised the fence on the inside path, where he showed Matt the cameras and emphasized the importance of ensuring that no branches or trees fell onto the fence and crushed it.

Matt and Liz dined as a pair for lunch, and they were relieved, to finally have an hour to rest. That afternoon they returned to the gym for self-defense classes. Sam, Liz, and Matt first learned their paces to figure out the breadth of their knowledge or ability on the subject as a starting point for their specifically tailored training schedule.

They all reconvened for an early dinner before Susan drove Mathew home. He was so exhausted that he fell asleep on the way. Susan helped Matt into the house, where she met his father. As Nat helped Matt into bed, he inquired, "What did you do to him?"

Susan took him outside. "We worked the hell out of him. Make sure you don't feed him breakfast. We will be taking care of all his meals."

"Why?"

"We have a nutritionist who will customize a menu for him. The teenage body responds to the stress applied to it to compensate, and we intend to transform him by the end of the summer.

Mr. Chambers gave her a funny look and repeated himself. "Why?"

Susan patted him on the shoulder. "We have our reasons, but we are going to make a man out of him---just watch."

Nat Chambers walked back into the house and reminisced about his youth when he decided to try to go out for the football team and began working out. He remembered how his body changed in just a few months. He and his wife had discussed getting Matt out for more physical activity, but she worried about her boy as any mother naturally would.

Nat felt a spark of that same enthusiasm that had prompted him to put all his efforts into getting in shape for the football team. He looked forward to the enjoyment of watching his son grow and transform.

CHAPTER 11:
Liz first driver's lessons

While Matt toured the fence, Trevor waited in the foyer for Liz as she exited the elevator. She approached Trevor in the typical, pouty, teenage fashion, "I hurt! Is it going to be like this every day?"

Trevor sympathized with his daughter, but he would not take it easy on her, "Well today your body is asking, "What the H E double hockey sticks is happening to me? But give it time--- we're not pushing you yet, and you will get used to it." Trevor could tell his daughter needed a change of pace and scenery, "Let's go for a ride."

Liz sighed in relief, "Good, I can rest."

They stepped outside and at the front door, and a car sat at the foot of the steps that was different from anything Liz had ever seen. It was low to the ground with wide-set tires, and the entire vehicle was just a frame encased in a roll bar. In the rear was a V-4 engine with independent fenders over each wheel.

Trevor walked to the driver's side and pointed to the helmet on the passenger seat, "Put that on and let me know if it doesn't fit." Liz was disappointed that she wasn't driving, but the car looked cool, so she nodded. She suddenly forgot about the overwhelming pain in her body. When she got in, she noticed that Trevor was putting on a five-point seatbelt. She needed Trevor's help to get it connected and adjusted.

Analyzing the seatbelt, she asked, "Is this necessary?" Trevor smiled and started the engine. He popped the clutch, setting off a quick squeal of the tires. Liz could feel the g-forces of the car accelerating forward.

They drove through the forest until they reached the racetrack on the Plantation. Liz felt lost and disoriented in the forest, but they eventually reached a clearing that opened into a dirt track. Trevor explained his next maneuver, "Now I'm going around the track slowly so we can make sure it is clear, but then I will accelerate and show you some of the driving skills you will need to learn, okay?" Liz yawned; she was tired from getting up so early to work out, and the prospect of sleep was more seductive than ever.

Trevor took pride in his daughter's drive and dedication. He popped the clutch into first gear, and the less than one-ton car with an engine producing more than one hundred and eighty horsepower abruptly leaped into the air, heading towards the first left turn. Trevor hit second followed by third gear at fifty mph. As he leaned into the turn at this speed, Trevor threw the vehicle into a sideways skid--- it slid into the corner right before he downshifted from third to second and hit the gas again. The engine roared, and the spinning wheels sent clouds of dirt up in grainy billows all around them.

The vehicle rocked back and forth in the corner and emerged at forty mph. Trevor quickly hit third gear before he moved left to set up for the right turn. Again, he shifted down and threw the car into another skid, this time going through the curve. Liz was now wide awake --- she was not expecting this level of excitement. She stared speechless at Trevor in shock and awe while grabbing the "Oh shit bar" and released a cathartic scream of joy.

The "Oh shit bar" is so named since grabbing the handles on the top of the inside car door was followed by an "Oh shit" statement. Trevor checked her quickly to make sure she wasn't scared and accelerated through the next turn. He sped down the one mile stretch into another left turn. Liz squealed in delight as Trevor powered through the curve and down the backstretch, which was three-quarters of a mile.

Liz's eyes were the size of saucers as Trevor turned the last corner and slammed on the brakes, skidding to stop where they had started. As the dust cleared, he asked, "Did you like that?"

Liz nodded excitedly, but Trevor had more to teach her, "We're not finished. "Trevor threw the vehicle into reverse and accelerated backward towards the turn they had just come through. Looking over his shoulder, he steered with one hand and burst out of the turn at forty mph. He headed into the back straight and revved the engine up to sixty mph. He spun the steering wheel to the left with a graceful flair and slammed on the brakes. The car twirled like a dreidel until the vehicle pointed in the other direction. Trevor shifted from reverse into first, popped the clutch, and wheels dug into the dirt sending it flying again.

Liz let out a high-pitched, "Yippee!" as the car sprang forward, flying off in the other direction. Trevor was now driving faster. He had only hit speeds of fifty mph before, but now he was well over eighty. When they finally arrived at the starting point, Trevor slowed down to a stop and shifted into neutral as they were engulfed in the dust cloud.

Trevor tested his daughter's mental endurance, "Still tired?" Liz remained wide-eyed and smiling as she focused on the road straight ahead. Trevor took her verbal cue, "That is some of what we will teach you. I wanted you to know what I expect of you. But for now, we will take it slow and just work on the basics. Let's change places." Liz couldn't get her seat belt off fast enough. She sprinted around the car to the driver's seat.

Trevor adjusted the seat and seatbelt for Liz's height and weight. After adjusting the idle of the engine from 600 rpm to 1200 rpm, he moved to the passenger and instructed, "Now, move your right foot up to your seat. You're not going to use it yet."

Trevor showed her the gear pattern on the shifter and told her to depress the clutch and let it out slowly, "Do you feel the change in pressure as you press it in and then release it?"

Liz affirmed, "Yeah, I think so."

Trevor put her hand onto the shifter and slid it into first gear. "Now let the clutch out slowly." Liz began to release the clutch but did it too quickly. When it began to engage, the car sputtered, and the engine died. She looked at Trevor who reassured her, "Start it and try again but let it out slowly." She did it again, and again the engine died once more.

Liz tried it several more times, but she became increasingly frustrated until finally, she blew. The pent-up rage from Jimmy Dittle was now creeping up to the surface---she needed a win today. She wanted to impress her new father with her driving abilities, but it wasn't working. She finally exploded in anger

She tried to rip off the seat belt, but her anger clouded her motor skills, preventing her from releasing it. She started pounding on the steering wheel and stomping on the floor until she finally tired, lying back against the seat and panting. Liz turned to Trevor and yelled in frustration, "What?!"

Trevor snickered. "Feel better? Good. Now this time, try pushing the clutch back in when you hear the engine start bogging down. As the clutch begins to grab, the engine will bog down, and the car will try to move forward. When you feel it, push the clutch back in."

Liz was shocked that he didn't get mad. Her eyes darted back and forth at his calm demeanor, she started the car, and of course, it died. Liz glanced at Trevor then started the car again and pushed the clutch back in. The car moved one foot! She smiled at Trevor and basked in her father's approval. On the next attempt, the car moved a few feet. She was getting it.

The hardest thing about driving a manual shift is the timing. As you let the clutch out, you must press on the accelerator at the right moment. Trevor was teaching her the feel of the clutch, and when it engages. She was mastering this skill, so he told her to move her right foot forward and accelerate when the engine bogs.

Now she needed to learn the timing of applying the accelerator to the sound of the engine, which was easier. She quickly advanced to the next step: shifting gears. It only took an hour for Liz to start from a dead stop and accelerate through all four gears. Once she made two circles around the track, Trevor stopped at the starting line and turned off the engine.

Trevor asked, "So how do you feel now? You have learned to get the car moving and shifting gears. Most people take a couple of days to learn how to do that."

Liz was smiling from ear to ear. "When can I drive around the track like you did?"

"You did very well today, but you haven't quite mastered starting and stopping. Once you do that, I will show you how to downshift into the corner and shift back up again. It will take time, but we will work on each part until you have it right---then we do crash and bang."

"What is crash and bang?"

"That is where we teach you how to ram one car with another to get through a roadblock."

"Really?" They were sitting where they came out of the forest. A left turn would head back to the mansion, and a right would take them back around the circuit.

Trevor tested Liz, "Okay, start her up, and let's head home. But I want you to go right, not left." Liz looked at him in surprise and went right. She drove around the track again, and when they reached the starting point, she turned left towards the mansion. When they arrived at the mansion, she was all smiles and covered in dust.

Sam and Matt were standing out front when Liz drove up. She jumped out of the car and bolted over to Matt and Sam followed by a cloud of dust. Sam and Matt observed Trevor as he exited the vehicle. Sam asked, "I take it she liked it?"

Liz tossed her helmet to Trevor, and he caught it. Matt pulled her into a hug and guided her into the building for lunch while asking, "So tell me what happened."

This was the schedule for each day. Winder school started at seven a.m. for the final week, and school ended on the third week of May. Trevor brought in tutors to prepare Liz for her finals. Trevor also negotiated a deal with the principal: new uniforms for the band and sports teams in exchange for leniency on Liz's absences.

When Matt arrived home from school, Susan picked him up and took him to the Plantation for his workout. After school ended Liz took over the role of transporting Matt to and from home. Liz didn't like having to get up at five a.m., but it was for Matt, so she gladly did it.

At the end of May, Liz and Matt exited the front door at seven p.m. to find Trevor standing in front of two Toyota trucks: the SUV they normally drove and a brand-new Tacoma.

They slowed to a stop, and Liz asked, "What is this?"

Trevor held up two key rings. "This key goes to the SUV that Liz will drive, and this key is to this truck assigned to Mathew. Make a choice."

Matt asked, "Are you saying that I get to drive this truck?"

"As long as you work here, you drive this."

Liz inquired coyly, "You don't want me to drive you home?"

Matt pulled her into a hug, "No, what it means is I now have a vehicle to take you on a date." Matt looked over at Trevor, "Can I take her to get ice cream, sir?"

"When are you going to bring her back?"

"It's seven now, so how about seven-thirty?" Matt beheld Liz's smiling face, "Want to go get some ice cream?" Liz jumped up and down and trotted to the new Tacoma.

Trevor handed the key to the SUV to one of his employees and went upstairs. When he entered the living room, Sam was sitting in the middle of the couch reading a book. She noticed him and asked, "Where is Elizabeth?"

Trevor pointed with his thumb over his shoulder, "Matt is taking her to get ice cream."

Sam sat up and looked harshly at Trevor, "Did you let him take her on a date?"

Trevor fumbled over his words, "No . . . he is taking her out for ice cream and will be back shortly."

"You still don't know how to negotiate with that girl."

Trevor continued glumly and picked up his book, "Matt said he will bring her back in a few minutes."

Sam looked over her book at him, "He'd better." Trevor sat down at the end nearest to the elevator, and Sam immediately moved over to sit next to him. Trevor pulled her close and kissed her. At seven-thirty-five, Liz came bounding into the living room, looking higher than a kite. Sam peered incredulously at her daughter over the top of her book, "Did you have fun?"

Liz could barely contain her excitement, "Dad, that new truck is so cool! We went to Hardee's for an ice cream, and he brought me back."

Sam scrutinized her daughter, "Where else did you go?"

Liz crossed her arms, "Nowhere else, mother. Matt told Dad he would bring me right back, and he did." Sam turned a page and nodded.

Liz then asked, "Matt asked if he could take me out on Friday?"

Sam looked up, "No!"

Liz stared at her in disbelief, "No! Why not?"

Sam continued to look at her book and appeared to ignore Liz, "Because he has to ask, not you."

With both hands on her hips, Liz demanded, "What is the difference between him asking and me asking?"

Sam lowered her book, "Because if a boy wants to take my daughter on a date, he needs to have the guts to come and ask me himself."

Liz frowned and tried Trevor, "Daaadddyy!"

Trevor raised his upside-down book to his face and said, "This is between you and your mother. I'm not involved."

Liz stuck her lower lip out, "Coward!" She stomped into her room and slammed the door.

Trevor asked, "Did I do okay?"

Sam smiled, "That, my dear, is how you deal with a teenage girl. Voila!"

Trevor was highly amused and impressed by Sam's mastery of reverse psychology, "So, are we getting together tonight?"

"Is that the only thing you care about?"

Trevor shrugged his shoulders, "I also care about dinner, but I'm not hungry…so yeah."

Sam gently slapped him on his leg, "You are terrible! I knew it!"

Trevor retorted, "What until we go to bed."

CHAPTER 12:
Sam gets some bad news

On Monday, Sam exited the elevator in the gray pantsuit from Louis Vuitton. Jamie exited the kitchen with a coffee and spotted her, "Whoa, hot Momma! What're you dressed up for?"

Sam rolled her eyes. "You remember this outfit . . . Nicolas gave it to me."

Trevor exited the kitchen and slowed to a stop, "Honey, you don't have to dress up for me. I like you in whatever you're wearing or nothing at all."

Samantha rolled her eyes again, "I need to go into Hutchinson and talk to Jennifer. We have several accounts that need to be completed, and I need to give my notice in person."

Trevor placed an arm on her shoulder, "You want me to come with you?"

"I can do this myself."

Jamie chuckled as she sipped her coffee, "That's right! You tell him, girl."

Sam smiled, "I will be back this afternoon."

Trevor replied, "Have fun!"

Sam and Jamie were excited to find her VW sitting out front. Sam lowered the convertible top. Jamie gave her a knowing smile, "I see you're wearing the thong again."

Sam was tying the scarf to cover her hair, "I see you noticed." They laughed as Sam pulled away.

An hour and a half later, Sam pulled into the parking garage and waved to the guard to let her enter. She exited the vehicle and headed toward the lobby while the guard watched her the entire way.

Sam was not the Samantha Raven he was used to seeing. Before, she personified the schoolmarm appearance. Today, she donned a Louis Vuitton couture that showed some cleavage. Her hair cascaded down her back, and she wore three-inch heels.

Sam cut her eyes to him with a Mona Lisa smile as she walked into the lobby and headed toward the elevator. Three men were already waiting for the doors to open then stepped out of the way to allow Sam to enter first. For the first time, she was being noticed. They pressed her floor before she could ask.

When she arrived at the fifteenth floor, Sam walked past the front desk and waved at Mary, the receptionist, as she passed. She could feel them watching as she walked to her cubicle with a small smile on her face. Sam began organizing her papers and mail on her desk.

After several minutes, Jennifer appeared at the opening of her cubicle, "Hi! Glad you came in today. Come into my office---we need to talk." Sam followed her and sat down on the other side of the desk. Jennifer sat down in her chair and put her elbows on the desk. She asked, "How are you doing?"

"It has been a whirlwind the past two weeks. I'm sorry for not coming to you earlier."

"It's okay. What your two friends did was great, and they saved me as they saved you." Sam remembers Jamie informing her that Jennifer was also caught in Rogers's web, so she explained everything that happened with Roger Dawson, Jimmy Dittle, and the reckoning of Susan and Jamie.

Mary rapped lightly on the door, and Jennifer motioned her in. Mary hugged both women and then looked at Sam. "Is that a Louis Vuitton?"

Jennifer looked at her in shock and asked, "It is! I saw it in the magazine. Where did you get that?"

Sam motioned for everyone to sit and told the story of going to the Plantation and confronting Trevor, learning that he was Tip, and having to wear his shirt after he tore her clothes off in his bedroom. This tale garnered snickers from the girls.

Mary's eyes grew large, "Oh my God, where did you go?"

Sam explained the shopping trip in Paris. Mary squealed and proclaimed, "You're kidding!" At that, Sam stood up and did a spin to show off the pantsuit. Mary and Jennifer laughed and cried before Sam showed finally them the engagement ring Trevor had given her.

Mary jumped up in pure excitement, "I knew there was something there. He came here to see you, didn't he? I just knew it."

Jennifer asked, "That was you who helped her change her look?"

Mary nodded, "I was watching from outside the board room, and judging from the look on his face when you walked in, I knew he wasn't here for the deal. He was here for you." Sam remembered that look and realized that Mary was right.

Mary apologized pre-emptively, "I'm sorry, but Mr. Bormann is here and wants to see you, Jennifer."

Jennifer told Mary to inform Mr. Bormann that she would be there soon. Sam waited until Mary left and asked, "Why is Bormann here?"

"I know you didn't mean to, but that day when I asked about Peterson's finances and you told me they used their savings as collateral, they jumped on it. Now they are trying to take over Peterson Corp."

Sam felt like she had been punched in the stomach, "Why do they want to see you? You're not helping them...are you?"

Jennifer shook her head, "They asked, but I told them no because I didn't have you. They were meeting today with another team, and I have this feeling that if they catch wind of your return, they might make another offer."

'What are you going to tell them?"

"I used you as my excuse to say no. Are you coming back?'

"No. Trevor wants me to work on his books and help him to get things in order."

"So, my excuse remains."

Sam nodded then looked off into the distance, "Thank you."

"It isn't that hard of a decision; you know we never did hostile takeovers before, and I don't want to start now."

"I think I need to go home."

Jennifer assured her, "I promise that I will keep you informed on what is happening." Sam nodded. As she was leaving, Steve Bormann walked out of the boardroom and greeted Sam with wide eyes, "Ms. Raven, it's a pleasure to see you. Are you coming back to work?"

Sam smiled and took his hand, "No, I just came in to see Jennifer."

"Well, I'm very sorry to hear that. We could use you on this."

Sam shook her head, "Jennifer and I never liked hostile takeovers. The only people who benefit are the pirates, and we don't believe that is good business."

Mr. Bormann's expression was saddened. "Well, some companies just outlive their usefulness, and they need to be culled from the herd---that is what we do."

Sam stood her moral ground, "It is not what we do."

She walked past Mr. Bormann and exited the building. When Sam got to the Plantation, she visited Gary and asked, "I need full access to the books. Peterson Corp. is under a hostile attack, and I need to get a handle on things."

Gary jumped into action, "Trevor told me to give that after you returned from Paris." Gary wrote something onto a piece of paper and handed it to her, "That is your login and password; let me know what else you need."

Sam nodded and then started to walk to her unofficial office, but first, she asked, "Is Trevor in his office?"

Gary had turned back to his monitor and looked over his shoulder, "No, he flew into Atlanta right after you left."

Sam halted and looked back at Gary, "Do you know what he is doing there?"

Gary stopped typing, "I believe he is meeting with some of the people we found on Jimmy Dittle's computer."

Sam nodded and made haste to her office.

CHAPTER 13
Trevor sets up the Charity

Right after Samantha left the Plantation, Trevor went back to his apartment and dressed in a suit. He made it to the veranda just as the helicopter was landing. Jamie and Susan were both dressed in white pantsuits, armed and waiting by the door.

As the machine finally settled down into the grass, they jumped in and headed off to Atlanta. It landed on one of the many tall buildings, and Trevor and his girls immediately headed inside.

They descended to the 20th floor, which was the Atlanta Paterson office. Trevor was dressed in his dark blue three-piece suit Jamie and Susan flanked him in off-white suits with red silk blouses. Both women had twin throwing knives hidden in the small of their backs in sheathes, ready for them to use with either hand to pull and throw in a moment's notice.

Trevor entered the 20th floor, which was owned by Paterson. The receptionist announced, "They are waiting, sir." Trevor nodded as they marched toward the boardroom.

They entered the twenty by twenty-foot room with a glass half-wall on the inside and a full glass wall on the exterior to find twenty-eight people waiting. As Trevor walked to the head of the table, several of the attendees stood to protest having to wait. Trevor stood at the end of the table and took everyone in.

At the far end was Jeff Morgan, who had come down earlier with the material that Trevor wanted to present. Behind him was a large document box containing nineteen sealed manila folders each, with the name of one of the attendees' presents. Trevor ignored the protest and locked eyes with Jeff, who nodded. Trevor looked around the room and held both hands up, "I apologize for being late, but if you please sit, I will explain why I requested your presence.

Trevor picked up a white paper before him and began. "I have an envelope for some of you that will explain everything." He began reading the names while Jeff and the rest of his team passed out sealed envelopes to each person called. Trevor instructed them not to open the envelopes until directed.

Afterward, Trevor announced, "Anyone who doesn't have an envelope before them, I need you to leave now." Several of the people looked up in shock and started to protest until Trevor raised his hands, "Please understand I don't think anyone with an envelope will want anyone else to see the contents. After we open them, those who feel they need their attorney present may request them, and we can invite them to a one-on-one meeting. But for now, I need everyone without an envelope to leave." Several of the attendees exchanged looks, and those without envelopes slowly rose and left.

Jeff walked to the glass interior wall and pulled the shades. He gave Trevor a nod as one of his men took up a position at the exit doors. Jamie and Susan backed away for a better advantage point to watch the attendees. Trevor looked at those left at the table and continued. "Okay, you may begin opening your folders. I must warn you that they contain pictures, so I recommend that you not pull them out or let anyone else see them."

The attendees, which included 17 men and two women, gave Trevor a suspicious look and then slowly began opening the envelopes. Several gasps could be heard throughout the room. These were the pictures that Elizabeth had found; in Jimmy Dittle's database, pictures of people he was blackmailing for having sex with minors.

An older man at the far end of the table stood up abruptly and demanded, "Where did you get these?!" Trevor extended a hand signaling for him to sit and allow everyone to finish inspecting their envelopes before he continued.

Once everyone viewed the contents, several sat back with white faces and covered their faces with their hands. Trevor glanced at his team and began explaining, "A couple of weeks ago, I'm sure everyone here saw the news reports of Jimmy Dittle and his little gang of rapists being taken down. There was a large fallout of peripheral items because of that. One was the fact that he had three houses with ten or more young women being forced into prostitution."

Trevor stopped to look at the people. "I know all of you are wondering what that has to do with me, so I will tell you. One of those girls was my daughter, and because of her, I gained ownership of his database, which also included those pictures." Trevor stopped to allow this information to settle into their minds.

The surly older man at the end of the table demanded, "So instead of us paying Jimmy our monthly club dues, we pay you. How much?"

Trevor smiled and surveyed the room once more. "Nothing." He looked at their expressions of disbelief and added, "I have two choices here. I could allow the police to gain access to these photos, which are damming enough. I can also use this information to do some good, with your help. I think we can make some positive changes."

The woman halfway down to the left looked at the men and asked, "I can explain how I got involved . . . ?"

Trevor held up his hand. "I'm sure everyone here has a story, but to be honest, it doesn't matter to me currently. My focus is on the rehabilitation of these girls. We all make mistakes, but how we correct them is what is important. Don't you agree?"

The woman remained frozen for several seconds. She scanned the others around before answering Trevor. "What do you have in mind?"

"Last year, I bought a hotel in Athens near the college. I was going to set it up as apartments for the college students, but I have decided to create the Abused Women's Center. I'm currently working with the authorities to have the thirty-plus girls in those houses transported to my hotel. What I'm asking from all of you is instead of me turning you over to the police, would you be interested in giving to my charity to help these girls?"

The old man leered at Trevor in utter disgust. "I understand that your daughter ended up in one of those houses, but that just proves she is just another whore like the rest of those girls." Trevor looked over at Jamie and could see she wanted to approach the man with ill intent, but he shook his head as a cue for her to hold off.

Trevor turned to one of the women sitting at the table and asked, "Ma'am, can you ever remember any women you have known in your life who wanted to be whore?"

She paused momentarily then said, "No, I can't."

Trevor confronted the man next. "I understand that it makes it easier to abuse them when you think of them as simple whores, but the oldest girl rescued was only 16---now think about that for a moment. These girls' range in age from 11 to 16. They became entangled in this horror show in various ways, but I assure you that it wasn't by choice. As responsible pillars of this community, don't you think it is our duty to right this wrong, and help them become productive citizens instead of continuing in the only life they know right now?"

The woman who was the target of Trevor's Socratic dialogue asked, "What is your plan?"

CHAPTER 14:
The Abused Women's Center

Trevor outlined his plan of housing the girls in his hotel and recruiting teachers to educate them. The next step included scholarships to UGA to release them from the imprisonment of life as sex workers and propel them into more productive fields. However, this venture required money, and Trevor had already donated his five-million-dollar hotel. He didn't tell them about the one million he had already stolen from Jimmy Dittle.

The crotchety old man spoke up again. "Just to clarify, you want us to pay for educating these girls. It sounds like a sweet deal---get laid for two years and then get a free ride to college."

Trevor did his best to maintain his composure with the delusional tormentor. "I don't know the individual reasons why these girls ended up in this situation, but all have missed at least one year of school---some as much as four or five. They are behind in every category and need help. If we don't do something, most won't make it to 21 alive."

The older woman looked down at the old man and asked, "What is your real problem with this? You can't handle a real woman, so you need a child to get your rocks off?"

The man started to say something when the other woman at the table interrupted. "Sounds to me like he needs his name turned into the police, or maybe you didn't hear Mr. Paterson say that instead of us going to jail, we have a chance to help these girls? We can't do that if we are in jail."

The old man pointed at the woman. "I have done nothing wrong."

Trevor corrected him. "Those pictures show otherwise."

The old man scoffed defiantly. "I was forced into this. The son-of-a-bitch had my son and told me that if I didn't entertain these ladies, he would deliver him to a pedophile. I was . . . trying to save my son; and ended up paying in blackmail."

Trevor nodded. "I have pictures of almost 40 people having sex with children. I called you people in because after studying the pictures in addition to studying your expressions and those of the children, I believed that all of you were coerced into those acts. I'm hoping I was right. If you don't feel the need to help, then you may leave. I will stick to my promise and destroy all the incriminating photos."

The man leaned back in his chair. "How much do you want per month?"

"These donations are up to all of you. As I stated earlier, I have already donated a hotel worth over five million. I also intend to donate more during the year. I encourage each of you to donate what you can, at least now, what you pay is tax deductible."

Another man asked, "What services do you plan to offer at this center?" Trevor motioned to Jeff, who fired up the big TV screen, showing the title page of a PowerPoint for AWC. Trevor presented the pictures of the hotel and began to explain via graphic renditions of the proposed plan. math, English, and history and later recruit trainers in other subjects. After the girls earned their GEDs, he wanted to transition into job training, offering courses in languages, cosmetology, medical training, and engineering. The old man remained closed-minded. "You think these girls will be interested in engineering?"

"It will be offered even if we only have one girl interested. I want to give her the chance, and I will be including legal training as well. They can become lawyers and policewomen if they choose to do so when they are ready to leave. My goal is to train them to carry out whatever they desire and realize that indentured servitude in the sex trade industry is not their only option."

Another male sitting at the table asked, "What is your estimate on the length of time they will stay at the center?"

"Excellent question! At this time, I think the average would be 3 years, but that depends on the girl, it could be as long as 10. One of the girls was taken when she was 10. She is 15 now, so she won't be legal for another two years. But consider the time missed from normal school. What if the girl wants to remain at the center until she earns a PhD from UGA or another college? I want them to stay for as long as necessary. Some will want to earn their GEDs, get a job, and move out; even then, I want to be supportive of what they want until they can stand on their own two feet. We have to understand the nefariousness of what they have survived. We as a community owe it to them."

The nineteen attendees glanced around at each other before one spoke up. "If I may speak for the group, I can see in everyone's eyes here that what you're offering is a valid and worthwhile endeavor. I will need to look at my situation to see what I can offer. Is there a minimum you need from us?"

"As we get this up and running, we can further determine the costs. We will be sending all supporters financial statements of the costs and balances in the checking account."

The woman to his left asked, "Have you secured someone to run the center?"

"Captain Fletcher of the Athens SVU has accepted my offer, and he is currently there setting up the security and organizing the facility."

The people silently regarded each other, and the second woman said, "I can't speak for the others, but I will be in touch."

Trevor smiled. "I included my card in your folders. I recommend that as you leave, make use of that shredder by the door to destroy the pictures."

The old man stared at the shredder. "What's to prevent someone from pulling the contents of the shredder and piecing the pictures back together?"

"That is a State Department-level shredder, and it will reduce the document to pieces no larger than 1/64 of an inch. You can check underneath to ensure the paper is sufficiently destroyed." The man walked over to it and began shredding his documents.

After everyone left, Jeff asked, "You want me to start visiting the others we found?" Trevor nodded yes. "Make sure you check them out thoroughly before meeting them. If you want to bring them to the Plantation, that is fine. If they give you too much grief, give the pictures to the police anonymously. I'm hoping that many will agree to assist us. This plan is going to cost a lot of money, so the more financial support we can get, the better."

Jeff gathered what material was left and departed with the two security men. Trevor looked at Jamie as she put her phone away. Jamie commented, "Our ride will be here in five minutes. If we are lucky, we will beat Sam home." All three left the boardroom and walked down to the CFO's office to meet with him as they waited for the chopper to return.

Trevor explained that the first floor was for offices and medical facilities, while the second floor would be segmented into classrooms and a gym. The third floor would be reserved for guests and employees to spend the night. The fourth and fifth floor was dedicated to housing the girls, with the sixth floor would be used as overflow. The penthouse would remain empty for now.

CHAPTER 15:
Samantha reacts to a threat

Sam opened a browser and began her research. She began with the stock exchange to see what Paterson Inc. was trading for. Next, she investigated the Bormann LTD stock and noticed that both stocks were rising in price. When activity for a stock increase, the value of the stock responds by going up or down. Because the stock values were going up, it meant that somebody was purchasing the stock.

Sam then checked her portfolio on Paterson and looked up the value of Paterson and the companies that it owned within the U.S. According to the portfolio, the company was worth well over 2 billion.

She remembered Trevor saying that his company was global, but only those assets within the U.S. would be shown in the portfolio. Those outside of the US would not be shown since Trevor probably placed those into different companies, which would be marked global or international. It was the same reason that there's a Google USA and a Google World. They were two different companies owned by the same people, but this setup enabled Google to separate the foreign assets and profits from those within the confines of the U.S.

The reason was simple. In 1993, Bill Clinton's new tax bill began charging taxes on profits made within the U.S. and outside if included within the same company. It didn't take long before every U.S. Company created separate companies for foreign and U.S. assets. The problem was that every company was already paying foreign income taxes to the country accruing the income but having to pay additional taxes on that same money was hurting the companies. Only the U.S. tax laws required this double taxation.

This bill didn't apply to foreign companies, which was why Chrysler sold itself to Mercedes Daimler, a smaller company. This tactic shielded them from several million dollars of taxes caused by regulations that were only applied to U.S. companies; also, it negated the requirements of having to do business with the UAW. The biggest problem with the UAW was that they didn't care for the company's bottom line. Their only concern was how much money they could pilfer from the coffers of the company.

Sam continued her research. She needed to figure out how Bormann was purchasing Paterson stock. She didn't think they would be purchasing the stock under their name. They would probably use some proxy purchasers so as not to alert Paterson to their intentions. As she studied the current sales, Trevor walked into her office." Hey! You're back."

Sam was nervous. She didn't want him to know what she had done, not yet anyway. She wanted to come up with an answer or plan before confessing her mistake. She faked a big smile and replied, "Yeah! Jennifer and I discussed some mergers she was working on, and she asked if I could look at them."

"Oh really? Would I be interested?"

"At this time, I'm not sure. You blew so much money on those other two companies.... do you have any money left?"

"I don't know. If the deal is right, I might be able to come up with something." Trevor was now leaning against the table that faced Sam, and he seemed to be enjoying himself. Sam was trying to hide her FUBAR (**F**ucked **U**p **B**eyond **A**ll Recognition) and was afraid of what Trevor would do when he found out.

Even though she had been upset with him before, now she knew who he was. She wanted him to love her, but could he still love her if she cost him his company---the company that had been started by his great-grandfather? The company his father once ran and now thrived under Trevor's leadership. Could he forgive her for doing that? Sam didn't want to take the chance--- daughter or no daughter, she couldn't take that chance.

Trevor started to walk across the office and Sam had to jump up because she didn't want him to see that she was researching his company as well as Bormann. She walked around her desk to meet him halfway. Trevor engulfed her in his arms, and she hugged him back. After he kissed her on the head, she said, "I promised Jennifer I would get back to her this afternoon, so if you don't mind, I need to concentrate. I can't do that with you here."

"Well, it is nice to know that I can still bother you. That makes my day."

Sam gently swatted him on the chest. "I'm glad I could bolster your self-confidence---now get out of here so I can get some work done."

Trevor then patted her on the butt. "Now I have something to look forward to."

Trevor left, and Sam went back to formulating a plan. Trevor had used the emergency savings as collateral for the purchase of the furniture and moving company, so that was tied up. She needed to figure something out at once.

As Sam delved into the details of Paterson Inc., she realized that if Trevor could buy Bormann stock by using money from the subsidiaries owned by Paterson Global, then he could backdoor Mr. Bormann. From what Sam could tell, Paterson Global had a lot more money in cash than Paterson Inc., even though she estimated Paterson Inc.'s value was well over 5 billion.

Sam thought about it and realized that to pull this off, she needed help, she needed to talk to the person who authorized the buying and selling of stocks. Sam went back to her notes and discovered that the person to talk to was the CFO. She found out that Dave Worthington was the Chief Financial Officer.

She found the listing and gave him a call. When Dave Worthington answered, Sam began, "Mr. Worthington, this is Samantha Raven, and I need your help."

Dave chuckled and asked, "Sure, how can I help?"

Sam began to explain and almost burst into tears. Sam was hoping that if she explained what happened, he would help her. Sammantha was scared, and the only way to make amends was to save the company. That would require his help.

She poured her heart out to him about everything: being badgered about how Paterson engineered the purchase of the two companies and the documents that outlined how he had achieved it. In a moment of desperation, she confessed what she knew.

She explained that she had figured out how to stop Bormann from taking over Paterson and needed his help. Sam was scared because she gave away the lynchpin that provided Bormann with the knowledge to try a hostile takeover. Trevor had just reentered her life, and she didn't want to lose him because she accidentally jeopardized his company.

Sam was at a loss for solutions, but she knew she had to dig into this. She hoped that she could either save his company or help fend off the attack. Sam wasn't sure what she could do, but she knew to come up with a solution, she had to understand both companies.

She explained that she had figured out how to stop Bormann from taking over Paterson and needed his help. Mr. Worthington confirmed her suspicions. "Yeah, I was seeing a run on our stock and wondered who was purchasing it."

Sam replied in a weak voice. "It's Bormann, but they are using proxies so that you can't tell who is financing the stock purchases." "Okay, so what do you have in mind?"

Sam began to lay out her plan. She wanted Mr. Worthington to use the foreign companies to start buying the Bormann stock and essentially do to them exactly what Bormann was doing to Paterson. She also recommended slowing down the Paterson buying process. Sam would begin looking at Bormann, to see if they have any subsidiaries, and match those to stock purchases. Mr. Worthington responded, "When do you think you can get me that information?"

Sam sighed. "I don't know yet. It all depends on if I can get the information?" "Okay, I will start the ball rolling on my end. I recommend talking to Gary. He can probably help you with that information."

Sam thanked him and hung up. She made her way to the control room and found Gary working on database search criteria. Sam pleaded, "Gary, I need your help."

Gary smiled at her with sympathy and understanding. "Whatever you need, Ms. Raven," Sam explained that she needed a list of all the subsidiaries of Bormann, and she wanted to cross-reference them with who was currently purchasing Paterson stock.

Gary eased her fears. "I can get that and send you the link to the information."

Meanwhile, Trevor sat in his office and heard his phone ring. He answered. "Hey, Dave. What's going on?" "Guess who just called me for help?" Trevor was expecting this call and chuckled. "She called, didn't she?"

Amused, Dave responded, "Yea, you said she would call, and she did. Should I do what she wants?"

"Is she asking to do what I suggested?"

"Yes, she is. I will start feeding her the information I have been feeding you."

"Thank you…and one more thing, don't tell her I know."

Dave laughed. "You must love getting your ass kicked by that woman."

"No, I just love the makeup afterward." They both began laughing as they hung up.

Sam had a lot to do and little time to do it. She felt that queasy feeling in her stomach that had been plaguing her for the last couple of days. She shook her head and thought to herself. This is not the time to get sick. Just hold it together.

CHAPTER 16
More for Sam to deal with

While Winder High was finishing its last week of exams, Trevor pulled in tutors to prepare Liz to pass the exams at the Plantation. The tutoring enabled Liz to get an A on all her tests, and she advanced to next year's sophomore class. Now that the school situation was resolved, he had to deal with her summer curriculum.

Liz would meet Jamie and Susan in the gym daily at six a.m. The routine would vary a little, but the goal was always the same. The nautilus machines got their hearts pumping and their bodies sweating. Pumping iron and other weight machines improved strength and range of motion. After that, the routine focused on splintering off according to what individuals needed to improve personally.

Trevor took Liz to the track every day to hone her driving skills while Matt inspected the fence. Lunch was communal, followed by a one-hour rest period. The tutors returned after lunch for afternoon lessons. Trevor decided that Matt could also use the tutors, so Matt was taking Spanish along with Liz. Afterward, Matt headed to the track with Susan or Jeff, and Liz worked with Gary on computers.

On Liz's first day with Gary, he sat down with her and began teaching her Assembly language for writing scripts. Scripts were small programs that could be keyed directly into a notepad file and then saved as a bat file, such as ping.bat.

Using the bat as the suffix made the file executable, and when typed, the file would perform or run the code within it. This allowed a programmer to enable or disable devices or connect to URLs and other devices.

Gary began working with Liz on how to key in the commands and run the bat files. Liz was fascinated by this technique because it opened the door to a computer world she had previously never envisioned. At three p.m., they all met back in the gym for another two-hour workout.

After stints on the treadmill or bicycles, they began to study fighting. Susan showed fight videos of Iron Mike Tyson. Susan said, "I want you to study what Mr. Tyson is doing and why in his youth, he was feared by everyone who faced him."

Mike Tyson was only five foot ten and around two hundred pounds. He was small for a heavyweight. George Foreman was six foot three and well over two hundred and thirty pounds, but even he feared Mike Tyson. Despite his size, Tyson could deliver so much power in his punches that very few men could withstand more than two or three before being knocked out.

Susan highlighted one of his fights against Donovan Razor Ruddock, who was six foot three and over two hundred and twenty pounds to pinpoint his technique. She explained how Mike was excellent at dodging the punches of the larger opponents as he stepped inside and delivered devastating blows to key points of the body.

Susan slowed down the video and focused on Mike's footwork, which was key. He would step in, placing his foot to push off for the punch. The power came from the foot. His body would be in a coil, and as he untwisted it, his leg straightened while his arm drove up into a punch to the solar plexus or chin with all the power in his body. They watched as Tyson fought Spinks---you could see the fear in Spinks' eyes as Tyson moved in. Spinks was knocked down in the first round and then knocked through the ropes from the center of the ring to end the fight. Donovan Ruddock made it to the seventh round, but the disbelief was visible on his face. How could such a small man deliver those blows?

Susan explained that even though both are crucial, technique is more important than physical strength. If physical strength were all that was necessary, then every weightlifter would also be a heavyweight boxing championship.

Susan and Jamie then began working with Matt and Liz on the speed bags, heavy bags, and focus mitts. These mitts trained them to strike a moving object with accuracy. Accuracy was integral to training since the target, like the solar plexus, was only the size of a silver dollar. To achieve maximum pain, one must nail the target.

Next, they focused on delivering kicks. Kicking with the legs was devastating to the recipient but also to the kicker. A poorly executed kick could cause one to break a foot or leg. Susan worked with Liz and Matt on Judo techniques and how to defend oneself against them. Most attacks on women occur in close quarters where the attacker can get close enough to wrap his arms around the female. Judo is the study of this form of fighting.

Liz wasn't enthusiastic about any of this. She didn't like to sweat, afraid that her body odor would put people off, but Susan and Jamie were adamant. Finally, Trevor called Liz in for a talk in his office. Trevor put Liz on the couch in his office with a laptop on the small table before her. Trevor leaned forward and placed his elbows on his knees. "You don't like the physical training?"

Liz gave a petulant look. "I don't see the need."

Trevor nodded and opened the laptop on the coffee table so they could both watch it. "When they snatched you off the street, how many men were you facing?"

"One. He grabbed me before I could do anything. Why?"

"You didn't move fast enough because you didn't know what to do. You had never been attacked like that before and didn't know how to defend yourself. But if you did know how to defend yourself, would you have been taken?"

Liz looked at him for a second. "He was larger and stronger than me, and there was nothing I could do."

Trevor opened YouTube videos of a young girl facing off against a larger man. It must be assumed that the man would be stronger and more adept at fighting since that is a natural part of being a man. But Liz watched as the girl took one step back then delivered a kick to his head and knocked him down. When he tried to get up, she kicked him again, and he was now out cold.

Trevor cued another video showing a young girl in an elevator with a much larger man standing behind her. When the man attacked her, she not only fought him off but also began to beat him mercilessly. When the elevator doors opened, he attempted to escape, but she grabbed him by his collar and pulled him back into the elevator.

She continued to beat him until the doors opened again, and he escaped with her on his heels. Liz looked at the videos in shock. Trevor smiled knowingly. "If that man faced you today, would you be kidnapped?" Liz's eyes grew larger as she realized what he was saying, and she shook her head no.

Trevor pushed the laptop over to her. "Watch some more." Liz watched several more videos of women defending themselves before Trevor said, "I can't force you to listen or work with Jamie and Susan, but you need to understand something. If that man had tried to kidnap one of those girls, what do you think would happen?"

Liz was staring at the still video. "She wouldn't have been kidnapped."

Trevor nodded. "I can put 50 men around you, but there will come a time that your safety and security will come down to you. You are the last line of defense for yourself and your family. Learning what Jamie and Susan can do isn't hard. It can be learned by anyone, but they must put forth the effort and practice to become proficient at it to use it. If you don't know what to do, you can cause harm to yourself. I have watched you in the gym, and despite your claim that you're a klutz. What I see is someone who can be very graceful when she chooses to do so. What I suggest is the next time you spar or work the heavy bag; envision one of those men in Jimmy's office. Hit back---hit them like you would like to."

Liz was looking at the video. "I don't like to think about what they did to me."

"Trust me, every time I think about what they did, I become infuriated. Don't think about what they did to you. Think about what you're going to do to them and let that be your focus." Trevor left her alone in his office. Liz watched a few more videos and returned to the gym.

Trevor walked into Sam's office. "I must fly to DC then New York and Spain. You want to come?"

Sam shook her head. "No. I've got a ton of stuff that must be taken care of for the wedding and the research for Jennifer and Liz. Did you talk to Liz?"

Trevor nodded and explained what had discussed with their daughter. "Only time will tell. I hope she does learn from Jamie and Susan, but it is up to her."

Sam hugged him tightly. "When are you coming home?"

"I should be back within a week." The next morning was Tuesday, and Sam watched his jet leaving. She had to step out of the SUV to throw up onto the pavement.

She held her upset belly and thought to herself. What is wrong with you, girl? You can't be doing this right now.

Sam drove back to the mansion and sent Jamie a message to come see her. When Jamie came to Sam's office, Sam asked her to close the door and sit down. Jamie was curious as to what was happening and looked at Sam, as she seemed a little green and sickly. Sam asked, "Jamie, can you take me into Winder so I can get a pregnancy test?"

Jamie's eyes flew open and almost bounced on the chair. "He didn't! He knocked you up already. Oh...that is so funny!"

Sam gave her a disgusted look. "No, it's not funny at all, but I have to know."

Jamie grinned from ear to ear. "Meet me out front in five minutes."

Before Jamie exited, Sam said, "Jamie, this is top secret. Tell no one." Jamie gave her a wink and left.

CHAPTER 17:
Sam's world is crumbling

Sam felt emotional and stressed about what was happening. She wasn't sure how Trevor would handle her being pregnant. Sam grabbed her purse and then headed to the front door to find Jamie sitting in the SUV. They jumped into the vehicle and headed into the forest. Sam looked over at Jamie, who had a wicked smile on her face. Sam angrily asked, "What are you smiling about?"

"You haven't been under his roof for a week, and he knocked you up again."

"I hope it's his."

"You think it might be Roger Dawson's?"

Sam laid her head against the headrest, working desperately to keep her tears from falling. "I wasn't on birth control, but he told me he had a vasectomy. So, I don't know. Then there was the security guy. Oh God! I just got him back into my life, and now I'm going to lose him." The hold on the tear failed, and one tear slid down her cheek.

Jamie reached over and patted Sam on the shoulder. "First, let's find out if you are pregnant. Then we can call our OB/GYN to the mansion to check you out."

"Excuse me? We have a what?"

"Trevor keeps several doctors on retainer who are willing to come to the Plantation, so we don't have to go to them. All the women who work at the Plantation use Dr. Cynthia Winston, partly because she is free."

"She was the doctor who saw Liz when he brought her here?"

"Yeah. Susan and I were in Atlanta rescuing you at the time. She would have been the one to see Liz."

Sam wiped her tears. "I need to thank her."

As they were leaving, Liz was watching from the highlighted windows on the right side of the front door and went to see Gary in the control room. "Gary, do you have a number I can use to call my dad?"

Gary smiled at her and showed her the phone book on the intranet. Liz wrote his number down, and as she was leaving, Gary asked, "Is there a problem?"

"Not sure yet."

Liz called her father from Sam's office. Trevor answered. "Hi, honey! How is it going?"

"It's me, Dad. I want to know---what did you do to Mom?"

Trevor was confused. "I'm not sure. Why, what is wrong?"

"She had been sick every morning for the last few days, and now she and Jamie just left, I think this is suspicious."

This bothered Trevor, and a sudden fear gripped his heart. He had been looking for her for so long, and now that he had found her, she was sick. He was going to lose her. "Liz, go to the control room and ask Gary to track where they went."

"What, you can track all the vehicles?"

"Yes, we can, but keep that to yourself. Okay?"

Liz smiled and said, "I'll get Gary to call you in a few minutes."

They hung up, and Liz walked back to the control room. "Gary, can you track Jamie and my mom?" Gary rolled to the computer on his left and brought up the motor pool list. He wrote down a number then wheeled over to the center computer and brought up a map on which he keyed in the number. In a few seconds, a blue dot appeared on the screen, and they watched it enter Winder down Route 81 and turn left into Walgreens' pharmacy. Gary dialed Trevor and handed the phone to Liz.

Liz said, "They just pulled into Walgreens." She heard him typing on his laptop. Liz asked, "What are you doing?"

"I'm checking your mother's credit card to see if she is using it."

"How do you have her credit card number?"

"Liz?" he asked quietly, but seriously, "Who am I?"

Liz gave Gary a strange look then answered, "Trevor Paterson, why?"

"I can do a lot of things that you can only imagine, and I do this to protect you and your mother."

Liz kept him posted. "They are leaving Walgreens now."

Trevor replied, "Jamie probably used her card---hold on." A few seconds later, Trevor asked, "So you say she has been throwing up lately?"

"Yes."

Trevor chuckled in relief. "Liz, I need you to trust me and not discuss this with anybody, but she is fine. Okay?"

Liz frowned. "What did they purchase?"

Trevor, with a smile in his voice, said, "Liz, I love you and your mother. I don't want to violate her privacy, so I need you to go to the gym and follow your schedule. You will find out when your mom is ready to tell you, okay?"

Liz didn't like this answer, but she acknowledged him and hung up the phone. She turned to Gary. "Can you check the credit card usage of Jamie?"

Gary gave her a questioning look. "No! I can't do that!"

Liz put on her angry face. "I will hurt you if you don't show me what Jamie just purchased at Walgreens."

Gary slowly turned to face Liz. "That would violate Jamie's privacy, and even though you could hurt me, she could hurt me even more."

Liz stepped closer and countered, "I'm going to tell Susan that you tried to feel me up unless you show me what she just purchased."

Gary shot Liz an evil look. "I'm so glad I don't have a girlfriend. He wheeled over to the computer to his right and brought up a URL. He signed in and rolled back to the main computer. "There you are." Liz sat down at the computer and clicked on Jamie's name as she smiled. She closed the window and said thank you as she skipped out of the control room.

Jamie was sitting in a booth in Friends Winder Grill just across the tracks from Walgreens. The waitress had just delivered their iced tea, and Jamie took a sip then glanced toward the women's bathroom door and waited. It took what seemed like forever, but finally, Sam exited the bathroom and slid into the booth across from Jamie. She extended her hand towards Jamie with a ball of tissue.

Jamie looked at Sam's expression and saw that she was strained and scared. "Did you use all three?" Sam nodded and looked away. Jamie unwrapped the tester and saw two pink lines. A big smile spread across her face when she looked at Sam who was now trying to control her tears and failing measurably

"Sam, hold it together."

Jamie pulled out her phone and dialed a number. "When is your next visit? Yeah, it is kind of important. I have a woman who thinks she is pregnant…Thank you." Jamie took both of Sam's hands in hers. "Now you listen to me before you lose it. This is not that bad. She will come tomorrow, and then we can be sure."

Sam took out a tissue and wiped her eyes. "I just found him. I can't lose him! Oh God! I have made so many mistakes."

Jamie pulled Sam closer to the table. "Samantha, the day he returned from that presentation, he was so happy that he was on cloud nine. He was terrified that he would do something wrong to scare you off. Since you have come to us, I have never seen him happier, so you get that idea out of your head right now. That isn't going to happen. Do you understand me?"

Sam nodded and repeated, "I just found him, I don't want to lose him." Her voice was strained but quite.

Jamie gave her a sly smile. "You would have to lose his company and get pregnant by another man to do that?" Sam sat back shocked with both hands to her face, and tears fell. Jamie moved from her side to Sam's side and slid close, pushing her back deep into the booth and demanded, "What happened? What did you do?"

Sam explained, "I was pressured on how Trevor had financed the purchase of the two companies, on the day I was rescued, I received a paper showing he had used his emergency fund as collateral. I unintentionally leaked the information to Jennifer, and now Bormann is trying to take over the company." Jamie grabbed her by the hand, pulling her out of the booth. Jamie tossed a ten onto the table and pulled Sam out to the SUV

Jamie stopped at the light across from City Hall and thought for a second. "Did you request that information?"

"Of course not. I did not need that information. It just arrived." The light turned green, and they proceeded through Winder.

When they reached the fork where 53 and 11 split, Jamie pulled off into the parking lot of Royal Blue Wine & Spirits and Rising Vapors and sat for a second. She looked at Sam. "If you didn't ask for it, then why send you sensitive information you don't need? Do you still have the envelope it came in?" Sam nodded yes, and Jamie headed to the Plantation.

Jamie pulled in front of the mansion. "Show me the envelope." They walked into Sam's office, where Sam retrieved the envelope from her briefcase and handed it to Jamie. Jamie inspected the envelope and the sending address. "Sam, come with me."

Jamie burst into the control room and hollered out, "Gary!"

Gary jumped up. "I didn't do it! I'm innocent, and you can't prove a thing."

"Bull! I want to know who sent this."

Gary stepped from the main computer. "Before you hurt me, let me see it."

Jamie handed Gary the envelope and winked reassuringly at Sam.

CHAPTER 18:
Sam puts things together

Gary looked at the manila envelope and then at Jamie. "If I don't tell you, are you going to hurt me?"

Jamie gave him a harsh look and very quietly replied, "Yes!"

Gary gave a pained expression. "I sent it."

Jamie moved right into his face and demanded, "Who told you to send that?"

Gary glanced at Sam and Jamie and replied with fear in his voice. "Trevor---he just came in here and told me to mail it. I had no idea what was in the envelope or why. I just did as I was told."

Sam stepped forward and asked, "When did Trevor know that Bormann was going to attempt a hostile takeover?"

Gary perked up a little. "Part of my job is running searches on who is purchasing our stock."

Sam gave him a quizzical look. "Why?"

"Because this isn't the first time Bormann has attempted this stunt. I was doing a query on our stock owners, and it showed that the same entities were constantly purchasing our stock---so I researched them. I found that they were all subsidiaries of Bormann."

Sam asked, "So you already had that list of stock owners, and that was why you were able to get it to me so fast?"

Gary nodded then glanced at Jamie and whined, "You're not going to hurt me, are you?"

"I haven't decided yet."

Sam held her hand up between them. "Gary, when did Bormann begin their attack?"

"About a month ago."

Sam looked at Jamie. "That was just after I came here. Jennifer asked me if I was willing to assist Bormann in taking over Paterson right after that. I declined, of course."

Jamie asked, "Why would Trevor send you that paper? He had to know that was the information Bormann wanted, but you giving that information to them would be unethical."

Gary spoke up. "Maybe because he wanted Bormann to try the takeover. Like I said, this isn't the first time they have attempted this."

Sam looked at Jamie. "And he needed for Bormann to think that Paterson Inc., was vulnerable. He needed the info to come from a source that Bormann would trust, so he set me up and just hoped that I would spill the beans. That is why Bormann is purchasing Paterson Stock. They don't think Paterson can offer a defense this time."

Jamie smiled. "Which means Trevor is tired of Bormann and has set a trap to take him down. He used you to leak the crucial bait to set it in motion. Now you know why I love that man; he can be so devious."

Sam was unamused. "But I don't like being used! He and I are going to have a word."

Jamie smiled mischievously. "Can I watch? I loved the last one."

Gary looked at both women. "You're not going to hurt me now?"

Sam stepped forward and patted Gary on the cheek. "Not this time, but if you ever keep any more secrets from me, I will ask my dear, sick friend here to talk to you." Jamie gave Gary a nefarious smile and followed Sam out of the control room. Gary sat down and wiped his brow.

Sam settled behind her desk, and Jamie pulled a chair, putting her elbows onto Sam's desk. "So, what are you going to do?"

Sam was rocking back in her chair and thinking when Susan knocked. "So here you are, Samantha. Do I need to be worried about you running off with my girlfriend?"

Jamie looked over her shoulder and smiled. "No, we just had to run a couple of errands."

Sam stared at her computer, trying to think of a plan. Jamie leaned back and said to Susan, "You won't believe what Trevor has done to her this time."

Sam gave Jamie a scared look as Susan pulled a chair over. "I'd believe anything short of knocking her up."

Sam shook her head aggressively and glared menacingly at Jamie. "He set me up to give potentially damaging information to Bormann so that they would try a hostile takeover. Now I have egg on my face, and I don't know what his plan is."

Susan smiled. "You can bet it is a masterful plan, and he will execute it flawlessly. By the time Bormann realizes what has happened, they will be toast."

Sam put her head into her hands. "I have an idea, but I need to find out some things before I finalize my plans."

Jamie looked at Sam, and with a giggle, asked, "Can you give a hint what you are going to do?"

"I need to do something that will teach that man not to toy with me."

Jamie squealed with delight. "Yes, something bold and daring! Neither man will ever forget what you're getting ready to do."

Sam had an idea, but everything had to go just right. For it to work, she needed to know how much stock each party had plus how venerable Trevor was. Sam had to make some calls and then run some numbers before working on her plan. She looked at Jamie and Susan. "Okay, I need to get to work, and you two get out while I scheme." They both laughed and walked out. She heard Jamie comment, "This is going to be great."

Sam called Dave Worthington again. "Dave thanks for helping me, but I just have a few questions?"

Dave chuckled. "Sure, what do you need?"

Sam used her quiet, shy voice. "After I talked to you last time, how long did it take for you to tell Trevor?"

Dave went silent and all she heard was, "Ah . . . " Sam then said, "Dave, if you lie to me, I will tell Jamie and Susan that you said they were too expensive to keep."

Dave stuttered again. "Ms. Raven, please don't do that. Everyone fears those two women."

Sam used her sweetest voice. "Thank you. Did you know that Trevor sent sensitive information to me that Bormann wanted, and now I can be accused of leaking that information to Bormann?"

"Ms. Raven, please. He told me he sent it, but I didn't like the idea. Please don't blame me."

Sam had him where she wanted him. "Under one condition: I want to take Bormann down so hard that they will never try this again and to show Trevor Paterson that pissing me off like this is not a good idea. Can I count on your help?"

"Is this going to hurt Trevor? He is my best friend?"

"It will scare him, but it won't hurt him."

"Count me in."

Sam was satisfied with her prowess. "I need to know who Bormann is using to finance their effort."

She heard Dave shuffle some papers before answering, "Morgenstern, that's right. Morgenstern International is financing them."

Sam smiled because she remembered that Trevor had told her he owned Morgenstern. "What has Trevor done in retaliation?"

She could hear Dave smile as he replied, "He has started purchasing Bormann stock."

"So, he plans to purchase enough Bormann stock in an attempt to own more of their company than they own of us?"

Dave chuckled again. "That is his basic idea." Sam thanked him and disconnected.

Sam then called Steve Bushier of Country Town Bank, who had worked in the New York Stock Exchange for ten years. "Steve, I have a stock market problem, and I need an education. Can I pick your brain?"

Steve almost laughed aloud. "Sure thing, Sam. What do you need?"

"I need to know how the New York Stock Exchange works with companies selling and buying stock."

Steve chortled in amusement. "Like all the other exchanges, it is controlled madness. The stock market is where companies buy and sell pieces of themselves in the form of stock that are then traded on the market or exchange. The value of their stock is displayed on a big board that is constantly updated. With the advent of computers, the speed of this process has greatly accelerated. What happens is when a new company pronounces its intention of offering stock in the company onto the exchange; they announce the date so the traders can investigate the company. When the day comes, an auctioneer mounts a podium and auctions off the stock. The value of the stock is determined by the amount of interest in the stock and the bidding. If there is an increase in demand, the price will rise, but if the stock is not selling, the price will hold or drop. The entire value is dependent upon interest and activity.

This was why when Facebook first offered to sell stock, the price fell after the offering rather than increased because it was not considered a good offer. It normally takes a couple of weeks for a stock to settle on its initial value, then it will go up or down from there.

When a trader purchases shares in a company, he gives the auctioneer a slip of paper showing the three-letter ticker name, his ID, and what he is paying for the stock. The auctioneer then records that exchange, and at the end of the day, the trader needs to pay for the stock he just purchased. All transactions must be completed by the end of the day, and the company must purchase all stock sold back to them. Today instead of a piece of paper they carry a tablet that is connected to the Stock computer network and record their intentions there.

Because all payments must be completed at the end of the day, there is also a requirement that the companies who trade on that exchange must keep a bank account on the premises so money can be transferred. The bank account does not need the maximum value of all the stock because most days, that figure is never reached. However, a certain percentage is required to complete the deal."

Sam asked, "Like what happened in the movie Trading Places?"

Steve replied, "That can happen, but you need to have a couple of traders in your pocket. Also, the Securities Exchange Commission takes a very dim view of that, if they catch anyone attempting to do it, they can be very harsh."

Sam then asked, "Let's say someone started trading hard on a company's stock. That could drive the value of that stock up, or maybe, if some news came out, that one company is taking over another company; there could be a run on their stock in the hope of benefiting from the merger. Is that correct?"

Steve replied, "If the target company is being taken over, the stockholders must be compensated by the acquiring company per stock value. Despite the size of the company, what matters is the value of the stock, if the acquiring company's stock is worth less, then they must give more of their shares to the shareholders in the target company. However, they need to make sure they have enough shares to complete the merger or takeover."

Sam thanked Steve and he requested her to call back if she needed additional information. Sam now knew what Trevor was going to do: he was having his foreign companies purchase shares in Bormann to become a major stock owner. Meanwhile, Bormann was attempting to purchase enough stock in Paterson to become the majority shareholder.

Both plans could work and have worked in the past. What Sam wanted to do was throw a monkey wrench into the deal and blow Bormann up.

CHAPTER 19:
The OB/GYN comes to the Plantation

On Wednesday, the OB/GYN arrived at the mansion, and Sam went to the medical center in the basement for her appointment. Dr. Cynthia Winston was a nice-looking blond woman in her forties, and Sam felt confident with her manner and professionalism. After the doctor checked her out, they sat for a private conversation. Cyndi was at her desk with Sam on the couch nearby.

Sam asked, "Okay Doc, what's the verdict?"

Cynthia smiled warmly. "First, call me Cyndi, and I think you are correct; you are pregnant." Sam dropped her head into her hands. She shook her head and sighed. Cyndi asked, "Not what you wanted to hear?"

Sam covered her face with her hands. "Do you have any idea how long?"

"After I run my test, I will be able to determine within a few days, but for now, all I can give you is an educated guess of just a few weeks."

Sam sat back in confusion. "I have waited for that man to find me for fifteen years and what's the first thing he does? He knocks me up! I'm not sure if I want to kick his ass or make love to him." Cyndi let out a loud laugh and shook her head. Sam sat for a second then asked, "You were the one who saw my daughter when he brought her here?"

Cyndi smiled and replied, "I'm sorry we didn't talk sooner, but other than a slight infection she was relatively fine...considering."

"At least she isn't pregnant like me. God, she spent a week in a whorehouse, and I have only been with Trevor for three nights. I must be a fertile Myrtle." Cyndi couldn't help herself and chuckled again.

Sam gave her an incredulous look and in a pleading voice, replied, "This is not funny. What if he doesn't want a kid right now? We haven't discussed this, and I'm just not sure."

Cyndi walked to Sam and sat on the couch near her, but not touching her. "I have known Mr. Paterson for several years, and every time anyone has a child, he is one of the happiest for them---but then he is sad when he sees the baby because it is not his. I don't know your story, but I know Mr. Paterson loves children."

Sam laid back against the back of the couch with a tear slowly running down her cheek and tried to smile. "Okay, but is he ready for me being all fat and pregnant? I'm scared."

"I don't think that is the problem. I think other things are bothering you. Want to talk about it?"

"Don't you have other patients?"

"No, not here. As you know I'm bound by my Hippocratic Oath, so spill the beans. Your future husband is paying me a lot of money, so don't waste it."

Sam looked down and chuckled nervously. "The money I've cost him already."

Sam needed to talk to someone. She needed unbiased advice. As she looked at the doctor, she decided that she might just be the one she needed. Sam began telling Cyndi about her first meeting at her house with Trevor, never realizing who he was. She relayed the stories of Trevor putting cameras into her home, bugging her phone, putting a GPS onto her, and the kidnapping of her daughter. Then she explained how she had leaked the very information needed for Borland to attempt a hostile takeover, and now she was pregnant. It was all happening so fast, and she was having a hard time keeping up with all the changes in her life. It was scaring her.

Sam also worried about Liz. She knew Liz was still suffering from Jimmy Dittle, and Sam was trying to be strong for her. Would Trevor forgive her for leaking the information? Would he think her getting pregnant was her attempt to ensnare him? When Samantha finished, the tears were again running down her cheeks. She had to bite her lip to control her emotions. She looked at Cyndi, who was sitting beside her, relaxed with an endearing smile on her lips.

Cyndi reached over and placed a reassuring hand on Sam's. "Samantha Raven, I have seen international models throw themselves at Mr. Paterson. He never batted an eye, which is why he hired two lesbians to guard him. I have seen the joy and sadness on his face every time he sees a young girl or boy with their father. He has looked for you for several years. I know because I had to run the DNA tests of mothers claiming their child was Trevor's and see the sadness on his face when I proved them false.

I also saw pride when he brought Elizabeth to me. Sam, I know this is hard to handle. Hell, Trevor is hard to handle, and I don't live with him. But have faith in your soulmate bond and everything he has done was for your safety. If he hadn't placed those cameras in your house, they would never have gotten the jump on who kidnapped Liz. If they didn't tap your phone, then how would they know where you were taken? If they hadn't put the GPS on you, how could they show up to rescue you? Yes, he violated every one of your rules, but he did do it for a good reason: he had finally found you and wanted to protect you."

Sam listened closely to the facts---the very same facts Jamie and Susan had iterated. She trusted them, but they were Trevor Paterson sycophants, while Cyndi wasn't. Sam then thought about him sending that information to her. She became momentarily lost in her thoughts.

Everything Trevor does is for a reason. He plans not for the day or month but for the year. His demands on health, driving training, martial arts, the language studies---they would all be beneficial down the line. When he hired Mathew to come to the plantation to exercise and train, it wasn't for what he had to do during the summer. It was for what he was going to face next year at school. Liz's driving lessons weren't for driving to the grocery store---they were for an occasion yet unseen. Therefore, the letter with the information was for something down the road as well. A smile slowly grew on Sam's face as all the pieces fell into place.

Sam realized that she was forced into a race that had started long ago with strategic players already in motion. There was no way she could just step into this race and run with everyone else. She had to start slow and come up to speed. Sam realized that she had been staring off into space and looked at Cyndi. "You must think I'm a basket case worrying about everything."

"No, I think you are a regular, overly hormonal pregnant woman who is worried about everything, particularly the fact that your man hasn't married you yet. Having your man legally obligated to you is a very comforting situation."

This time, Sam laughed aloud. "I never looked at it like that, but yes, you're right."

"I think Trevor has already told me the wedding is in two months—August, I think?" Sam nodded with a smile. Cyndi continued, "I hope I will be included in the small gathering, but I suggest this: keep to what you can control, like the wedding. Accompany Trevor to the meeting with Borland. You will learn a lot from that. Don't worry about not remaining abreast of everything. Trevor has been doing this for a long time and is very good at what he does. He must be, because every time I come here, there is always something going on. In time, you will realize that you have a handle on everything, just like him."

Sam got up and looked at her belly. "You think I will be showing then? Oh God! I just pictured myself waddling down the aisle like a white hippopotamus."

Cyndi rose, placed her arm around Sam's shoulder, and guided her to the door. "Most women don't start showing until the sixth month, and the end of July will be about your third month. So other than being overly horny and hormonal, I don't think you will have any of those issues."

"I wasn't overly horny with Liz."

"You weren't sleeping with her father then. That man can make my grandmother horny."

Sam had to cover her mouth to muffle the giggle. "Yeah, just looking at him sometimes gives me all kinds of dirty thoughts. I thought I was developing a dirty mind."

Cyndi stopped at her door but didn't open it. "I'll tell you some of the things my other patients have said. I had a good Christian woman and church elder, tell me she was so horny when she was pregnant that she wished she could clone her husband and make another one so they could both take her at the same time."

"Oh my God! I don't think I could handle two of them. He's almost too much now."

Cyndi chuckled again. "I had another patient tell me she bought her husband a prescription for Viagra and a six-pack of Red Bull. She put Viagra into his food and had him drink Red Bull before going to bed. I saw him just before she delivered, and he looked worn out from no sleep. He told me he was so glad she was delivering because he couldn't last much longer." They both laughed as Cyndi opened the door and guided Sam out into the small office.

Cyndi then said, "Instead of you coming to my office, I will bring the results here on Friday. I want to be here for that lunch." Sam hugged Cyndi and left the office. She got to her office and sat down at her desk when Jamie and Susan both knocked once and then stumbled into her office.

Sam had to grin as Susan looked back out into the hallway, making sure that no one was around. She shut the door and locked it. They brought the two chairs to her desk and looked at her with expectant eyes. Sam looked at both girls and asked in exasperation, "What!?"

Jamie started. "Well, give us the news! When, who, what is it?"

"Human and I will know on Friday."

Susan looked at Jamie. "It was Thursday when she was screaming from the third floor...a girl."

Jamie shook her head. "No way! When she returned from Paris after blowing a quarter million on clothes, she would have been more receptive...a boy."

Sam's mouth dropped open. "Excuse me, but Jamie, you were sworn to secrecy! Now you're making bets on when I was conceived?"

Susan laughed. "That does sound better than being bred, but I can go with it."

Sam whined, "How many know---the entire Plantation?"

Jamie and Susan began counting their fingers before Jamie replied, "Not even half. We haven't told anybody."

Sam took a serious tone. "Don't tell Liz yet."

Both women laughed. "Who do you think told us?"

Sam covered her face and looked to the side for thought. "Well, Cyndi said she is coming back Friday to bring me the results."

Susan confirmed with wide eyes, "She is coming back on Friday?"

Sam gave them a quizzical look and asked, "Yeah, why?"

"She will be here in the morning so that she will be invited to lunch to watch the show."

"What show?"

Jamie looked at Sam as she and Susan rose from the chairs. "You will be making the announcement, of course. We all want to see what Trevor is going to do."

They started to the door when Susan said, "I bet he will stand and take full credit."

Jamie chimed in as they exited, "No, that is a safe bet. I bet he will order cigars and whisky for everyone."

Sam sat back in her seat with her mouth open in shock and shook her head as she thought. Trevor Paterson, what have you gotten me into?

CHAPTER 20:
Sam learns the facts

Dr. Cynthia Winston came on Friday to the Plantation and directed Sam to the examination table, where she rubbed some gel on her belly and turned on the sonogram equipment.

Sam was on the examination table with Jamie on one side and Cyndi on the other seeing if they could find the baby. Finally, Cyndi proclaimed, "I think that is it." She took some measurements and consulted a chart. "From the test and what I'm seeing here, the fetus attached to the uterus about three and half weeks ago. That would make the day of conception on this day here."

Jamie and Sam both looked at the calendar. Sam laid back and released a sigh. "Thank God!"

Jamie had a devious smile on her face. "Yep! The day of your come to Jesus' moment."

Cyndi chuckled and asked, "Day of what?"

Jamie nodded and explained, "That was the day Sam realized that Trevor had bugged, videoed, and GPSed her and came back to the Plantation to kick his ass."

Cyndi was still chuckling. "Classic! You were screaming at him?"

"I was also punching and kicking him in his office until he told me who he was."

"You didn't know?"

Sam tried to explain. "In college, he was thinner with long hair and beard. He looked nothing like he does today, and when he told me, I was in shock."

Jamie spoke up. "Yeah one thing led to another---she fainted, and he carried her up to his apartment."

Cyndi held up a hand and said, "Wait, this is getting good. Let me sit down for this." She pulled up a rolling stool to sit down.

Jamie then continued to explain. "Well, he takes her up to his apartment while the rest of us were with Liz on the Veranda for dinner, when suddenly, we heard all this yelling, screaming, and a whole lot of "Oh My Gods" from the bedroom window."

Sam gave Jamie a disgusted look. "That wasn't my fault either."

Cyndi snickered. "No, it wasn't, honey. It was his."

Jamie then continued. "Liz tried to go up twice to rescue her mother, but Susan and I convinced her that she didn't need saving."

Cyndi laughed and covered her mouth with her hands. "Oh my God."

Sam nodded. "It gets better."

Jamie kept relaying the story. "About thirty or forty minutes later, they finally walk out onto the veranda, and she is wearing one of Trevor's Guayabera shirts."

Cyndi asked in shock, "What happened to your clothes?"

"They didn't survive---neither did my panties or bra."

Cyndi was holding her hand over her chest. "That had to be embarrassing?"

Sam nodded. "It gets worse."

Cyndi looked at Jamie, who continued, "Well we convinced Trevor that if she was to stay at the Plantation, she needed clothes, so he gave us his credit card to go shopping."

Cyndi smiled and replied, "Of course, it was his fault."

Jamie laughed. "So, we are shopping, and Trevor calls me and says we have to get Sam and Liz out of the country. He instructed us to come back and go to the landing strip where a plane would be waiting."

Sam interjected. "I get out of the car and ask---what is this? And the only thing she would tell me was that the store wasn't here, and we needed to fly there. I figured it was just in another city."

Jamie smiled and added, "It wasn't until after we took off that I told her we were headed to Paris."

Cyndi's jaw dropped. "Oh, that is good, wait . . . did you have a passport?"

Sam shook her head. "No passport, no toothbrush, and the only clothing I had on that was mine, were my shoes."

Cyndi almost fell off the stool. "Only in a book or movie could this happen."

Jamie then said, "So we get to Paris, and an old friend, Jacques Dubonnet, was waiting. He cleared Susan and me, but all Sam had, was her driver's license, and Liz only had a library card."

Sam spoke up. "He looked at us like we were crazy and asked why we had come. Liz said we came to go clothes shopping, and the frightened little thing handed over her library card."

Jamie was hysterical at this point. "He chastised Sam for wearing Trevor's ugly shirt and told her she should give it back or burn it. Jacques is an old friend, and he just wanted to have some fun with her," Cyndi was now doubling over laughing.

Sam recalled her embarrassment. "I wanted to crawl under a seat somewhere."

Cyndi continued laughing and asked, "What happened then? Did you go shopping?"

Jamie smiled; she loved this. "We hit Louis Vuitton, and of course, they just loved Trevor's shirt! They gave Sam an outfit to leave in instead of that shirt. Then we hit Susan Ricci and about four others before coming home."

Cyndi looked at Sam trying to hold her side from laughing. "Well, serves him right, for knocking you up. Are you going to announce it now? I want to be there for this."

Sam sighed and rubbed her belly. "Might as well get it over with."

That morning, Trevor had arrived home, unpacked, and walked out to the Veranda for lunch. The talking was going a mile a minute until they saw Cyndi, Sam, Susan, and Jamie exit onto the Veranda, and then a silence settled over the group.

The silence was thick like a blanket covering the entire table as everyone just passed the food around and gave each other side glances, trying to ignore the elephant in the room. Sam sat down on Trevor's right with Liz and Matt on her other side. Everyone was doing a poor job of acting normal and not talking, which was not normal. Matt was lost.

Finally, Sam glanced at Cyndi and loudly asked, "What is going on here?"

Everyone stopped whatever they were doing and looked at each other. Gary replied, "Lunch?"

Sam crossed her arms and looked around the table then angrily. "You were talking up a storm until we walked out, then everyone shut up. Something is going on. What is it?"

Trevor had taken a slice of ham and rolled it up with a slice of Swiss cheese. He was taking bites and asked, "Cyndi have you got any interesting news for us?"

Cyndi gave Sam a sly smile. "Why yes, I do. You won't believe who is pregnant now."

The entire table went silent, and everyone first looked at Sam then Cyndi waiting for her to finish her statement. "Mrs. Thompson is in her second month."

Jamie's eyes went wide. "Did she get her husband another prescription of Viagra?"

The entire table erupted in laughter and a few shot side-glances at Sam. Gary said, "I know what I'm giving her husband, Jack Daniels. He is going to need it." Sam looked around the table as everyone kept avoiding the burning question in their minds but didn't want to be the one to bring it up.

Finally, Sam shook her head and said, "Okay! I have an announcement." The entire table erupted with Trevor standing up yelling, "Yes!" Everyone was clapping and pointing at Trevor, who had his arms extended and was smiling with excitement. Sam looked at them in shock and bellowed, "I will be going with Trevor to the Bormann meeting. I think it will be an interesting learning experience." She glanced at Cyndi, who was attempting to quell a snicker.

Trevor sat down slowly with shock and disappointment on his face as he looked at Sam then nodded slowly. "It will be very boring, honey, but I think you're right. It could be a learning experience."

Sam nodded and looked at everyone, who went back to eating. No one looked up except for Cyndi, who was sitting on the other side of Trevor, supporting her head with one hand, and watching Sam with a smirk on her face. Finally, Sam quietly said, "And yes, I am pregnant."

Everyone suddenly looked up at Trevor, who glanced at Sam and stood up with his arms outstretched; twisting from one side to the other like a sign making sure he showed his front to all the observers. He pounded his chest with everyone clapping and pointing at him. He then proclaimed, "I did it!"

Sam looked at Cyndi, who was now sitting back and chuckling as she watched the show. Trevor ordered, "Consuela, whisky, and cigars for everyone."

Sam took her knife and tapped it on the side of her glass of tea. "Consuela, stop. Trevor, sit down, and Liz, I will deal with you later."

Liz gave a painful smile. "Sorry, Mom. I was worried because you were throwing up all the time. I called Dad and asked him what he did to you."

Jamie piped up declaring, "He knocked her up again, that's what he did."

Sam waved a finger at Jamie when Susan asked, "Do we have a conception date?"

"It was the day, of my come to Jesus' moment, as Jamie would say, from the apartment."

Liz squealed, and Susan held her hand out to Jamie. "Pay up, sucker!"

Jamie pulled a dollar from her bra and handed it to Susan. "Do we know the sex?"

Cyndi spoke up. "It is too soon for that."

Trevor leaned over and quietly asked, "You okay with this? Are you happy?" Sam sat back to think, and yes, she was happy. She had dreamed of this day for fifteen years: having her man back, sharing his bed, making love to him, and bearing his children. It is that relationship between a man and woman coming together and merging their strengths and weaknesses, bringing children into this world, and making a home and family unit, that is the core of all societies. And the most important accomplishment is teaching those children to become contributing members of society.

Sam had so many times felt alone and helpless, trying to ensure the safety and growth of her daughter. Today she looked around the table at her new friends who had pulled her into this family despite her reluctance and made her feel at home. For the first time in a long time, she felt wanted, loved, and cherished.

Sam looked up at Trevor, smiled, and nodded yes.

CHAPTER 21:
Samantha Finding Herself

Sam looked over to see Liz gazing at Matt, who was looking around the table in shock. He had never experienced this type of elation. These misfits comprised a more closely-knit family than some real families did, probably because these people never had one. Now they were basking in the glorious confluence of the exuberant joy of this family. Sam made a mental note to talk to Cyndi about birth control for Liz. She could see the adulation of love in her eyes.

The chatter around the table continued about the upcoming birth and wedding as they wined and dined. Sam felt blessed to be a part of this family. Now she had to confess her wrongdoings to Trevor, even though she knew he was already aware. However, she had a plan to draw out a confession.

After the announcement, Sam and Trevor disappeared into their bedroom. Sam made Trevor sit on the side of the bed as she picked up a manila envelope and stood before him. "I need to confess something, and I want to apologize."

Trevor studied her as she continued, "A week after I finished helping you, someone approached me about helping Bormann execute a hostile takeover of Paterson Inc. They wanted me to divulge information about your company to achieve that end. I refused, of course. One of the questions was how you financed the purchase of those two companies, and at the time, I didn't know. A few days later, I received this manila envelope with the very information they wanted, but I did not need it. Can you explain why this ended up in my hands?"

Trevor scratched his chin. "Bormann has been trying to take me down for about eight years now. This was their third attempt."

Trevor soon realized that he had just pulled the pin from Sam's rage grenade and tossed it. She stepped closer to him. "So, you decided to involve me?!"

Trevor smiled sheepishly. "They knew you had just spent three days here going over some of my books, so they would think you knew how it was done and pressure you to secure that information."

"Is that why you kissed me, hoping that I would fall madly in love with you and not give any of your secrets away?", "No! Of course, not...no!" He tried to use his sad, puppy-dog eyes on Samantha. "I had been looking for you for so long, and I realized that you didn't know who I was. I needed to know if you still loved me."

Sam raised her chin in defiance. "Did the kiss tell you that?"

A smile slowly replaced Trevor's solemn expression. "Your eyes hadn't realized who I was, but your heart knew. I felt that in your kiss. I wanted to tell you at that moment, but I had been advised to proceed carefully."

Sam jabbed him in the chest. "So, you decided to use me instead?"

Trevor's smile faded as he leaned forward and placed his forearms onto his knees. "Yes and no. I realized that you would be the best source of that information, but I had numerous doubts and reservations. Later, I worried I had violated your trust."

Sam crossed her arms over her chest again. "I wasn't going to tell them anything. I even made sure the document was safely secured in my briefcase. That last day, I was so upset because I couldn't reach Elizabeth, all because of you! I didn't want to go to see Roger, and when Jennifer came into my cubicle, I screwed up and confided in her. Later I learned that Bormann was trying to take over Paterson, and I was afraid you would hate me for that!"

Sam vehemently waved the folder in Trevor's face. "Then I learned that you sent me this. How am I supposed to feel about you using me this way?!" She couldn't even look at him right now. Trevor slid off the bed and slowly approached Sam from behind. She turned and backed up, holding her hand out to stop him. "Don't touch me; I want to know why you used me like that?!"

She kept retreating to avoid Trevor as he slowly pulled his shirt off and stepped out of his shoes. Sam was enticed and infuriated. "Don't! I don't want to see you naked, and we are not having sex until I get some answers."

Trevor simpered devilishly. "I wanted the information to come from you, and I knew you would be under pressure. I also know that an accidental leak was a possibility. That way, Bormann would think they could take me over, and I could spring my trap." Sam turned away from him again, struggling to resist him. Every time he touched her, he reignited an eternal flame that had burned softly since the day she met him. She needed to have this out before she gave in---this argument wasn't over just yet.

Sam snuck a peek at him out of the corner of her eye, and all he had on was his undershorts as he continued to pursue her around the room, finally cornering her beside the bed. He closed the distance between them and began touching her. Sam tried to push his hands away, but he forcefully pulled the duvet from the bed, picked her up, and pulled her onto the bed as she writhed beneath him, trying to escape.

Trevor pinned her hands over her head, kissing her neck and nibbling on her ear lobe. As he unbuttoned her blouse, he whispered, "I didn't want you to be aware of my plan. I knew you would be furious, and you are so hot when you're mad at me."

Sam wriggled her right hand free and hit him on the back as he pushed her bra aside and assaulted her breast. She gasped. "You are not fighting fair right now."

Trevor retorted, "When do you fight fair?" Sam vainly tried to get her breast away from Trevor's mouth because it was begging for his attention. She felt his other hand moving down to her belt. He opened her slacks and plunged his hand down into her nether regions.

She haphazardly demanded, "Please stop. I'm not through being mad at you." Trevor gave another low chuckle that resonated to her very core as he released her left hand. Her right hand and arm were stuck behind him. She used her left hand to try to push his head off her breast, but his fingers found the quintessence of her body. After working his way down into her pants, the shock wave shot through her. She grabbed his forearm to pull it up, but she wasn't strong enough. She enjoyed this interplay of voluntary submission. Every time she pulled; his fingers wrapped tighter around her core. They would rub against it, which turned her on even more. Sam hissed in desperation, "You bastard."

Trevor continued feasting on her ear and sucking on her neck, sending shivers down her body that crashed into the shock wave coming from the other direction. Trevor changed tactics and decided to take her clothes off. He jumped up and grabbed the top of her pants and yanked them off.

Sam took the opportunity with his hands off her and sprang up and hit him again in the chest. She pushed him back and declared, "Now stop! There will be no sex until I'm satisfied." Trevor looked at her wearing nothing but her bra and panties and smiled.

Trevor begged, "What if I satisfy you first and then confess?"

"No!" Came her command, she knew the penalty of giving in too quickly.

Trevor knew he had lost the advantage, so he tossed her pants aside and conceded. "Okay, whatever you want."

Sam composed herself momentarily, "I have a plan to take Bormann down. Since it was partially my fault, I want to execute my plan."

Trevor sighed in defeat. "Tell me your plan." Sam pointed to the overstuffed chair and motioned for him to sit. Once he was seated, he sat back to study Samantha. He was immediately aroused by her, and Samantha noticed.

She sauntered towards him, working her hips to the max, and gradually removed her bra and dropped it on the carpet. She only left her thong, and settled on top of him, straddling his lap.

She clutched a handful of his hair as she leaned forward with her breasts inches from his mouth and explained what she wanted to do. Trevor tried several times to suck one of those breasts into his lips, but Sam kept a firm hold of his hair, thwarting his futile attempts.

When she was finished, Trevor felt every small move she made in his lap and could just taste those nipples in his mouth. "You diabolical little vixen, you! I like that plan. I will call Dave and tell him to follow your instructions." She smiled at Trevor, who glanced up at her and with a smile, "May I?" Sam smiled and released her hold of his hair.

Trevor dove into her ample bosom like a starving man who has not eaten for weeks. He took her to the carpeted floor and made short work of her panties. They never even made it to bed. Trevor pulled her close. "I want to apologize for underestimating you."

"Just don't do it again, or I'm cutting you off for a week."

"That is cruel!"

"So was the way you used me."

And so, the summer continued. Matt and Liz dedicated four hours every day to the gym. Jamie worked with them on other aspects like sword fighting and knife throwing. Matt was good with his hands, but Liz was a natural with knife throwing.

Matt grew taller and stronger every week with the diet plan and work schedule. Even Liz gained a few pounds, and her strength, endurance, and shape made leaps and bounds in improvement. However, she abhorred physical exercise and sweating, and neither she nor Mathew realized the changes in their bodies just yet. They had seen each other every day so to them they were still the same as the first day.

A few days before school started, Trevor called both Liz and Mathew into his office for a talk with Sam and himself. "In a few days, you two will begin school. Matt, you will come here to get Liz and head to school; neither of you must disclose what you have seen here or what I do. I'm invisible, and I like it that way."

Liz was somewhat in tune with her father's frame of mind. Matt asked, "Are you afraid of people knowing how rich you are?"

"Yes, that knowledge only leads to trouble. I like being innocuous. If everyone knew who or what I was, I wouldn't be able to drive my truck or go to the store. It would make me a target, and because of that, you two would be targets as well. I don't want that."

Matt asked, "So, you are her father, and anything beyond that is unnecessary information?"

The curious expression on the teenagers' faces incited nostalgia in Trevor. "When I was young, like most kids, I wanted to be rich and famous. My father took me to meet some of the rich and famous people I idolized. I realized that they existed in gilded cages. If they wanted to drive to the store, go to a high school football game, or just go driving around on a Friday night, it was dangerous because people would jump in front of them and sue them for money. I cherish the ability to partake in the simple things that regular people take for granted. If my financial status became public knowledge, I would be inundated with requests, threats, and lawsuits."

They both nodded yes. Elizabeth realized that if the truth of her father was realized then his problems would soon become hers. She understood that his request for anonymity not only benefited him but her as well.

CHAPTER 22:
Change can be good

The showdown with Bormann finally arrived. Samantha flew with Trevor into Atlanta and landed on the roof of his building. They exited the elevator into the lobby of the Paterson Inc. office. As he approached the receptionist's desk, she announced, "They are waiting in the conference room, sir."

Trevor's face showed all business as he just nodded and breezed through the entrance. His corporate lawyer and CEO were waiting; they fell into step behind them as Trevor marched past. No words were shared; this was business---serious business, this was war.

Trevor wore his Brook Bothers black three-piece suit, and Samantha flanked him in a white, Louis Vuitton business suit showing just a hint of cleavage. Her hair was in its customary bun, and she carried her briefcase as she kept one step behind Trevor. As she exited the elevator, she pulled her cell and speed dialed Steve Bushier, "How are we doing?"

Steve chuckled and replied, "I haven't had this much fun in years! It's exhilarating. They started buying Bormann stock at the bell and watched the value rise steadily. When do you want to start the sale?"

Sam smiled. "We are entering the board room in two seconds, so I think now is a good time." Steve Bushier had two stock traders who had spent the last week buying Borman Stock. They would now have a fire sale of the Borman stock which would force the Borman stock to drop in value. Steve also had two stock traders representing foreign companies, owned by Paterson International to purchase that stock. At the reduced price they were purchasing as much stock as possible.

"Consider it done." They disconnected. Trevor had slowed slightly and was listening to Sam's side of the conversation. They glanced at each other, no other signal was given, and both knew the plan.

They entered the boardroom to find Steve Bormann sitting on the other side of the table with his lawyers and people. Bormann LTD consisted of five men all looking serious and confident that their efforts would be successful. Of course, why wouldn't they? They had always succeeded in the past until they attempted to take over Paterson. There was no reason to think that today's outcome would be any different.

Two weeks earlier, word got out that Bormann LTD was attempting a hostile takeover of Paterson LLC. Since then, the market trading of both companies has been strong. The initial stock values showed that Bormann had more expendable capital than Paterson did, predicting that the takeover would be successful. During the last week, the demand for Bormann stock was going up. Consequently, Paterson stock declined as more people continued to sell their shares in hopes that they wouldn't lose any money. It didn't look good for Paterson LLC.

Trevor took the seat directly across from Steve Bormann while his CEO sat to his right. When they entered, Samantha stepped behind Trevor so that Trevor and CEO were the first two seen as they entered the room. Sam stepped from behind Trevor to sit directly on his left. Steve had a confident smile as she watched Trevor Walk in, but it quickly faded when Sam stepped out and sat beside him.

Steve was no fool; he knew Samantha was brilliant and having her sitting on the other side scared him. He looked to his left at his two accountants and hopped that they were up to the task. They had calculated that they had the majority shares and would be successful. The accountant showed Steve that Borman stock had been going up in value, the selling of the stock gave Borman more money to purchase Paterson Stock, his plan was working.

Trevor sat down in his chair. There was no customary exchange of handshakes. This was war but not with weapons or armies per se. It was war in the business world, where there was no loss of life, but the stakes were still high.

Sam sat down, only shooting a fleeting glance at Steve Bormann, and pulled her laptop from her briefcase. She connected to the stock exchange and pulled up her notes on what needed to be accomplished during this meeting. Sam gave a small smile then looked up to see Steve Bormann watching her.

The Bormann/Paterson contingent was seated on the opposite sides of the conference table. At the end of the table, the mediator sat to Trevor's right. He was a retired judge who had performed as a mediator for Bormann on several occasions. What Steve Bormann didn't know was that Trevor had supported him when he was selected to sit on the appellate court. However, Judge Downing was known for being a no-nonsense judge and took great pride in being fair and unbiased.

The judge opened the meeting by announcing, "I will now call this meeting in session by saying for the record that Bormann LLC has called this meeting to perform a hostile takeover of Paterson LLC on the grounds they are now the majority shareholder. This of course will also require an election of a new president and board members of both companies."

The judge then looked at Steve Bormann, "Mr. Bormann, you will provide the evidence that supports your assertion, that you own the majority number of shares of Paterson LLC?" Bormann looked to his right, and one of the accountants removed several pieces of paper, which had a list of entities who owned Paterson stock along with the amount of stock they owned. The list was given to the Judge and Trevor who looked at the list and then at the bottom figure that showed the total number.

The number of shares they owned, along with what Mr. Bormann now owned constituted 34% of the total shares of Paterson Stock. Trevor was fully aware of what they owned and knew that their 34% was more than his 29%.

CHAPTER 23:
Setting the Parameters

Mr. Bormann glanced at Sam, who was busy typing out a message on her phone. He then addressed Trevor, "Well Trevor, it appears that the jig is up. I told you I would own your company one day, and that day is today."

"Well Steve, I wouldn't count your chickens before they hatch. We still must pick a new CEO of Paterson and Bormann."

"Since I own most of the Paterson Stock that makes me the de facto President of the company. By the end of next week, it will not exist."

Sam looked up at Steve Bormann and interrupted. "We have to agree on some items before we go forward."

Steve Bormann looked at Samantha and then back at Trevor. "She speaks for you?"

Trevor replied, "She speaks for herself, but I support what she says."

Sam glanced at Trevor before turning back to Bormann. "I want it stipulated that there will be no golden parachutes."

Mr. Bormann smiled. "Agreed!"

Sam then continued, "We want to stipulate that no supermajority will be allowed during the finalization of this merger." Mr. Bormann smiled again and agreed again. He figured that with his majority shareholdings, those concessions had just ensured his victory.

Sam didn't smile or indicate any intentions. "During the merger, we will not stagger the board of directors."

Mr. Bormann leaned forward. "Since this is a takeover and not a merger, as you like to call it, I don't have to agree to anything. But that does appeal to me."

The judge interjected. "We are here today to set the parameters. It doesn't matter that the marriage is consensual or not, but we need to know what each party expects and if it is agreeable to the other."

Mr. Bormann gave the judge a disgusted look. "It doesn't matter what the parameters are. We will take over the company, keep the pieces we like, and sell the rest. There is nothing they can do about it."

Sam kept a straight face. "We would like to have a list of all of those entities you used to purchase Paterson Stock so we can confirm that it was done so legally."

Mr. Bormann shook his head. "I just gave you the list."

The judge spoke again. "You have to report the acquisitions and verify that they are legitimate."

Mr. Bormann looked at the judge and then back at Samantha. "There are no others involved?"

Sam continued to study him. "I want to note that since Mr. Bormann has stipulated that there are no other entities involved with him on this other than those on the list, then no other entity can be produced during the final meeting." Mr. Bormann and his team conceded through a series of gestures.

The judge continued. "A verbal response is required, Mr. Bormann."

"Yes, who do you want us to submit the list to?"

Sam leaned back. "I recommend Hutchinson accounting. Since they aided you in this hostile takeover, you shouldn't mind." Mr. Bormann looked at Sam for a second then turned to the two accounting personnel beside him and nodded.

The judge spoke again. "Give me the information, and I will carry it to Hutchinson personally. That way, we can all be assured it will arrive." Sam nodded her acceptance.

The judge announced, "Okay, I have an opening in one week. If it's satisfactory, we can meet on that day and complete this proceeding. How say you both?"

Trevor looked at Mr. Bormann and nodded. "That will be agreeable."

Mr. Bormann gave him a big smile. "That is good for me."

Everyone exited the boardroom. The Bormann group headed down to the street while Trevor and Sam headed to the roof and the Paterson group headed to their offices. Sam pulled her cell and made a call. "The records are on the way." She disconnected and then boarded the helicopter.

When Mr. Bormann reached the lobby, his accountant had just disconnected from the drivers of their limousine and informed Mr. Bormann, "It will be here in two minutes."

Mr. Bormann turned to his lawyer. "Do you think she knows?"

The lawyer shook his head. "How could she? I know you said she was good, but no one is that good."

Mr. Bormann nodded. "I don't care. Put security onto those three companies and I don't want any slip-ups this time." The lawyer nodded then stepped away so he could make a phone call as the limousine appeared.

CHAPTER 24:
Sam sets her trap

When Sam arrived home, she walked immediately to her office and called Jennifer Wills, who confirmed, "We are going through the entities now. We already compared the companies to those on the list Gary gave us, and we are now checking those companies that purchased the most shares."

Sam replied, "Thank you, Jen. Can you send the top ten to me? I will see what I can learn from here." Jennifer agreed, and within minutes, an email appeared in Sam's inbox with the list.

Sam was hanging up when Elizabeth walked in. "How can I help?"

Sam copied the bottom five from the list and printed them as she said, "I need to know who and where these companies are. Are they capable of purchasing the Paterson stock they just purchased?"

Liz picked up the paper. "I'll get Gary to help me and see what we can find."

Liz exited the office and headed to the control room. As she entered the control room, she pulled some tape from the dispenser and taped the paper to a monitor. "Gary, we need to check these companies and determine if they were really able to purchase the amount of stock they purchased."

Gary looked at the list. "You start on the top one, and I will work up from the last one." They began searching. They had worked for several hours when that afternoon, Gary turned to Liz and said, "Hey, I need to call it quits. I'm seeing double." Liz looked at him and whined, "This is dad's company, and we have to get this done." "Yea, but I've been working since seven, and I'm beat."

Liz patted him on the back. "Go ahead and crash. I will keep at it." Gary walked over to the couch and lied down to sleep. Liz continued until near midnight.

Sam came into the control room and glanced at Gary on the couch. She walked over to Liz and laid a piece of paper on the console. "I did a quick query on these companies, and these two here look suspicious."

Liz looked at the two companies then pointed to the first company she had on her list. "I looked at this company here and noticed that it spent almost one million on Paterson stock. Last year, their gross income was only $400,000. My first question, if they only grossed just under half a million, how did they come up with one million to purchase the stock?"

Sam and Liz looked at each other then asked at the same time, "Is it legal for Bormann to give money to other entities to purchase stock for them?"

Gary spoke from the couch without opening his eyes saying, "No, it's not, but why would a company do that to begin with?"

Liz asked, "How long have you been awake?"

Gary smiled and replied, "When Samantha walked in wearing that perfume and whispered---that is an immediate wake up call."

Liz scoffed. "You pervert. You've been pretending to sleep so you can watch my butt as I work."

Gary sat up and rubbed his eyes with the heel of his hands. "Now not to say that you don't have a very fine butt that is worth watching, but no, I was asleep, and I can't see your butt with my eyes closed---but I can smell your mother's perfume with my eyes closed, so I'm not a pervert."

Sam smiled. "Okay. Then giving money to a company to act as a proxy to purchase stock isn't illegal, but that is going to take resources and effort of the proxy. So why would they do it?"

Gary lay back against the sofa. "Most entities won't put out that much effort…unless there was something in it for them. They must watch the market, ensure the stock they bid on cleared, and then record the amount of stock they have. That takes a lot of effort. It could be beyond the financial capability of some companies. I think you need to start looking there."

Sam asked, "Why would a company want to do that?"

Gary shrugged his shoulders. "The reasons are as numerous as there are people. Maybe they have a beef with Trevor. Maybe Bormann is forcing them to do it. The only way to find out why is to hack into their system and look at their financials."

Sam and Liz gave each other tired looks. Both had been at this for over seven hours when Gary stood up from the couch and glanced at the clock. "Okay, I have had about six hours of sleep. Liz, would you mind getting me a cup of coffee? I will start looking at those three companies you found."

Sam asked, "What do you want me to do?"

Gary had just finished stretching and replied, "Go and crawl in bed with Trevor. I don't want him down here in the morning all grumpy because you spent the night with me."

Sam smiled. "He won't be grumpy." Gary gave Sam an incredulous look. "Bullshit. He spent 12 years looking for you, he didn't do that to wake up alone. Now get out of here so I can get to work." Liz gave Gary an angry look at Gary and said, "So her butt is better looking than mine?" Gart gave a huff and said "Yes!"

CHAPTER 25:
Gary Makes an Interesting Discovery

Gary looked at the three companies and performed a search on the New York stock exchange, only to find that they were not on the stock exchange. Next, he checked their websites, and only one had a website. These were small companies that didn't use or need the internet for their business, except for one, Rollez. He then pulled every news article with the name of any of those three companies and began reading through them.

The only company that had more than a couple of news articles was Rollez. Rollez was born in Virginia Beach to a dentist who loved sailing his small catamaran along the shore. He had a Hobe Cat, which was very popular, and since he lived on the beach, he pulled it up on the beach near his house. The problem was that it required several people to move.

After some experimentation, he discovered that by employing large, fat, lightweight wheels under each pontoon, he could move the boat by himself. After a couple of design flops, he came up with a working design. The idea took off, and many of the Hobe Cat owners who had boats on the beach wanted a set.

The dentist invested some money to build sets of the wheels and sold them to other sailors with boats on the beach. He then realized that the wheel design had more uses and began designing other uses, such as wheelbarrows, that became instantly popular. That was when he realized that he had to contract out for the parts. He signed a deal with another company to manufacture the plastic parts he needed to assemble his product.

That was when things started to go sour. The plastic injection company that was manufacturing the parts was owned by Bormann LTD, and they saw a bigger market. However, they had to get control of Rollez first. They began by getting the Dentist sign a noncompete contract. That way he had to purchase the parts from them. They then started slowing down the delivery of the parts, causing the company to default on some deliveries. This situation caused financial difficulties for Rollez, and since he was locked in to only purchasing parts from this company, he was stuck in a no win position.

To stave off bankruptcy, he agreed to purchase more than 9 % of the Paterson Stock that Bormann was using to gain a majority. This also meant that he was an unwilling partner and had no allegiance to Bormann.

Gary quickly saw the correlation between the Rollez stock purchase and the timely delivery of the parts he needed to fill his orders. Gary couldn't help but feel he was only delaying the inevitable, because as soon as Bormann gained control of Paterson, he was going to seize Rollez.

This was the ugly side of capitalism. A famous line by President Herbert Hoover, an orphan who went from rags to riches because of capitalism, stated, "the only trouble with capitalism is some of the capitalists; they're too damn greedy." Mr. Bormann could have collaborated with the dentist, but he wanted total control and used a non-competing contract to steal his company.

Gary then looked at the other two companies and found the same scenario being played out. The next morning when Liz and Sam came down, Gary had stories to tell them. Sam asked, "I need their personal information so I can contact them." Gary handed over three folders with information on each company.

Sam gave Gary a hug and walked with Liz back to her office. Jamie and Susan walked in. Susan stopped and looked at the serious expression on their faces then asked, "Is this a mother daughter discussion? We can come back."

Sam shook her head. "No stay! I need some ideas." Jamie shut the door and locked it. Susan jumped onto the table beside Liz while Jamie pulled a chair over and sat down.

Sam explained what Gary had revealed to her. "I need to go see them personally. What I need them to do can't be explained over a phone call. I need to meet them face to face."

Jamie rested her head on her arms across the back of the chair and looked at Sam. "Who do you want to take with you?"

Susan spoke up. "Mr. Bormann will be watching these companies, and if Trevor shows up with us in tow, he will know it. Obviously, you can't go by yourself."

Sam looked at both women and nodded. "I agree, but who can I take with me?"

Jamie looked at Liz, "Take Liz, and Jeff."

Sam looked at Liz. "What do you think?"

Liz responded sheepishly. "I don't know a thing about being a bodyguard."

Jamie smiled. "Listen to Jeff. He will clue you in. Just keep a angry look on your face and watch everyone."

Liz looked at Susan who just nodded. She turned back to her mother. "I'm not sure, but I'm game."

Jamie looked at Liz seriously. "All of the men on this plantation already hate sparing against you. Just remember what we have taught you, and be angry, very angry. The rest of it will take care of itself; besides, no one will try anything with Jeff along. He is just too damned big to bother with."

Sam sighed. "Okay, I need to do some digging, and I will set up our trips. Liz, go talk to Jeff, he will probably want to go over some things you will need to know and understand before we go." The three women nodded, and Liz followed Jamie and Susan out of the office. Liz found Jeff in his office and filled him in on what was happening.

Jeff rocked back in his chair and studied Liz for a second. He was pondering how Liz was going to handle this. He leaned forward. "Let's go to the gym. We will need Mathew in on this."

CHAPTER 26:
Summer ends... and So does Bormann

The Bormann takeover backfired, as Jamie had predicted. Bormann was spending large amounts of cash and had almost emptied their coffers to purchase Paterson stock via proxies. Furthermore, Sam found Bormann didn't own the companies. She realized that they were doing this because Bormann was blackmailing them. Three of the biggest purchasers were a construction company in West Virginia, a ship builder in Norfolk, and a plastic company in Virginia Beach. Sam contacted each company and arranged a meeting in Charlottesville, VA.

Trevor Paterson was known for his organizational skills and his ability to bolster company profits. Most companies took advantage of a long-term relationship with Trevor as opposed to making a quick buck. They accepted the synergistic relationship with Paterson and signed a contract to receive investment capital and management aid.

When the time came to complete the takeover, the three companies voted with Bormann LLC to assume ownership of Paterson LTD---this meant that Bormann had to pay for Paterson stock by issuing Bormann stock. This was where they began to fall short.

What Bormann didn't know was that Sam had worked with Steve Bushier, who contacted several of his friends on Wall Street. The meeting began with an announcement that Bormann did show ownership of most of the shares and that made them the primary owner. A good part of those shares were owned by other people who were voted with Bormann.

This made Steve Bormann happy. Now Steve had to issue Bormann shares for Paterson shares owned by Paterson Share owners. But because of the decrease in the value of Bormann Shares this meant he had to issue more shares than he initially intended.

Because of the drop in Bormann stock, this caused a sale of Bormann stock. The sale of Bormann stock, which took a massive nosedive in value from $75/share to less than $10/share. Consequently, Bormann had to cover the buyback of their stock with cash. They also had to cover their loan to Morgenstern by surrendering more stock to Morgenstern as payment. In short, Bormann didn't have sufficient stock or funds to trade for the Paterson stock.

Mr. Bormann's last hope was to be voted President of the new company. This is where the three companies Sam had talked to had bought 25% of Paterson shares now owned by Bormann. But they voted for Trevor instead of Steve Bormann. The value of the voter is held by how much stock in the company they own. The companies from Paterson global along with the three companies Sam had met with, and the shares that Trevor now owned after Bormann had bought his shares of Paterson Inc. constituted most of the shares.

Morgenstern demanded that Steve Bormann sign the loan as the guarantor of the loan with his personal wealth. When Morgenstern demanded repayment of the loan. Bormann didn't have the funds to repay the loan. So, Trevor bought his shares at a cut rate price. This put Trevor as the owner of most of the shares of Bormann LTD. Steve Bormann broke. He never realized that Morgenstern was owned by Paterson Global.

Trevor quickly made short work of Bormann LLC. The earlier decision of, no golden parachutes or mixed boards, which Steve Bormann had agreed to, came back to bite them big time. Suddenly, he and his board were unemployed.

Companies like Rollez, who were being pressured out of their business, realized that the plastic injection company that was squeezing them, was now owned by Paterson. They had a new investment deal with Trevor Paterson to expand their company.

Trevor looked at Sam. "You are brutal, and I love you." Sam gave him a pensive smile. "I want you to remember this moment the next time you try to use me without my permission." Trevor gave a bigger smile. "Oh, I will---I will."

In early August, Trevor and Sam married at the Plantation, and the five of them traveled to Spain for two weeks at his olive oil plantation. Matt remained behind because he was trying out for football team. He had failed the two previous years.

Matt's transformation that summer were dramatic, to say the least. The five-ten, one hundred eighty-pound boy with 30% body fat had grown into a six one, two-hundred-and-ten-pound man with broad shoulders and only 1% body fat.

Trevor and Sam returned just a week before school started so Liz could get ready, and Mathew used his truck to take her to school. Liz didn't realize her transformation until she returned to high school. During study hall, her friend, Tara, asked, "What have you been doing to yourself this summer, and why haven't we seen you or Matt?"

Liz smiled and didn't quite know how to answer. "Well, my dad found mom and me, and we moved in with him. He is kind of an exercise nut, so I guess that would explain my summer."

Tara looked shocked. "Oh! So, your mom got married. Did you take Matt with you?"

Liz chuckled. "My dad hired him to work at his house."

Linda was sitting on the other side and said, "Well, whatever he is doing it is doing him good." She touched her friend's arm. "Have you seen him? Oh my God, has he changed!"

Tara looked at Liz. "You look really good too, and that outfit, your mother is getting good at making clothes!"

Liz didn't want to reveal that the pants outfit was an original design for her from Ralph Lauren, so she replied, "She is getting good."

Everything was going well until Wednesday of the first week. Liz was at her locker trading books, when suddenly, her door slammed shut, and a tall young man with blond hair was standing in front of her with a smirk on his face. He turned to his two friends, "Yeah! You're right---it is her!" He molested Liz with his eyes." I hear you spent some time this summer in a whorehouse. How about we get together later, and you can teach me what you learned?"

Liz was a little intimidated, but she wasn't going to turn her back. She just stood defiantly and looked at the young man with a straight face. Suddenly, Matt appeared; he shoved himself between them and pushed the tall, blonde boy back. When one of his friends stepped forward, Matt grabbed him by the back of his head and slammed it into the locker---the boy slumped onto the floor. When the second boy stepped forward, Matt caught him and spun him around, and held him with his arm outstretched but twisted backward. He held him at arm's length as he said, "Elizabeth is with me, and anyone who messes with her answers to me."

Matt tossed the second sycophant into another locker and looked menacingly at the tall blonde. "Do we have a problem?"

The boy held both hands up in surrender. "No problem." The two boys rose from the floor, making sure they kept their distance from Matt, and followed the tall boy down the hall.

Liz glanced up at Matt in shock and awe. She had seen him develop during the summer but seeing him do this was shocking. She calmed herself and asked, "Who was that?"

"He's the quarterback, and he is in love with himself. I will have another word with him this afternoon at practice." Liz looked up at Matt with a slight smile when she heard, "Hi Matt!" Two girls walking by were giving Matt the eye. Liz glanced at them and looked back at Matt, whose eyes were firmly on her. She asked, "Who are they?"

Matt gave her a questioning look, "Who is who?" He looked up and down the hall then back at Liz.

Liz smiled and retorted, "Nobody." She walked with Matt to her next class.

Matt had grown two inches and gained thirty pounds of muscle. The self-defense courses also improved his balance and speed. He was no longer the pudgy Matt; he was the hard-bodied, chiseled, handsome Mathew Chambers.

The previous year, Matt did not make it past the first cut, but this year, they had a new defensive coordinator who claimed Matt as his center linebacker. Matt took to the position and quickly began to learn the ins and outs of defense. Matt enjoyed exploding through the offensive line and blowing up any play before it had a chance to develop; he was stronger and faster than most of the other players.

After the confrontation in the hallway, Matt wanted to reinforce what he had said earlier. That afternoon at practice, during the scrimmage, Matt blitzed. The QB received the ball, looked left, and pretended to throw the ball. He turned right only to find Matt sacking him hard. The offensive coach was furious since the QB was wearing a red shirt. As Matt got up, he whispered to the QB, "Just making sure you got my message."

The QB gave a grimace and nodded, "Yeah, got it!"

That Friday was their first game, and the team they were playing didn't have a decent offense. Because of Matt and the new defense, Winder was able to pin them near their goal line. Winder was able to win by kicking two field goals! This was the Winder QB's second year, but he still telegraphed his throws. He was tall with a powerful arm, but he wasn't very accurate. The Winder team had improved since the previous year, but they didn't believe in themselves and hadn't realized their potential. Most of the defense was Matt plowing through the line and obliterating plays before they could get started.

Winder's next opponent had a better offense and was able to drive down the field in the first half and kick two field goals, which gave them a six-to-nothing lead. Late in the fourth quarter, a Winder punt placed the other team on their ten-yard line.

All the other team had to do was run out the clock to win. However, after two running plays that netted them negative yardage, they were desperate to gain a first down to remain in control of the ball. They tried an earlier play that had been successful. The QB threw back to a wide receiver lined up on the outside, who then threw it downfield.

When Matt saw the formation, they placed a wide receiver to the right with two other receivers in front of him to block. Matt switched positions with left cornerback, and when the play began, he was hit by the first receiver, who tried to block him. Matt threw off the attempted block, and when the QB threw the ball back to the wide out, Matt ran in front of the receiver, intercepted the ball, and carried it into the end zone. This extra point kick by Winder gave them a seven-to-six lead along with the victory. Winder had lost all but two games during the previous season, and now, because of their defense and Matt's effect on it, they had won two games already.

Gainesville was their next opponent. Winder was a two-touchdown underdog, but that Monday, everything would change.

CHAPTER 27:
The QB made a bad decision

The following Monday, Elizabeth had just completed her first two classes, and now she had a study hall before lunch. When she moved to the Plantation, she reluctantly began working out with Jamie and Susan. They were working with Liz on several methods of protecting herself. Jamie was a Win Chun master and several other martial art forms, Susan had multi-black belts in Judo and Kickboxing as well as several other Martial art forms. Liz had been training for four months, with physical exercise, the training affecting her.

Liz pulled out two books and a notebook, then closed the locker then started down the hall. Today she was wearing a tight dark blue sweater with semi-loose jeans and steel-toed boots like what Jamie and Susan wore.

The Study Hall was at the other end of the hall in a classroom, whose door was across the hall from the back door to the rear of the theater. As she turned the corner of the hall and headed toward the door of the study hall, two arms collapsed around her and lifted her off the floor.

One arm surrounded her chest with one hand covering her mouth so she couldn't scream, and she was at once carried through a door into the back of the theater. Liz tried to free herself, but her arms were not strong enough, finally, she was placed on her feet on the floor in the rear of the Theater. The entire area was dark except for the single light in the ceiling as she watched the QB who moved into sight.

The strong arms deposited her on the floor about six feet from the QB who was standing in this QB jersey and blue jeans and a smirk on his face. The QB finally said, "Now that we are alone, we can get to know each other." The hand moved from her mouth and Liz countered, "So does your friend have to hold me or are you afraid of me?" The QB motioned with his chin, and the arms unwrapped from her, and she could feel the person move back. Liz glanced over her shoulder and found the three-hundred-pound center standing behind her with his arms crossed.

Liz realized her situation, but instead of being scared, she remembered what Jamie and Susan had taught her, to evaluate the situation, analyze who and what they are, wait for the opening, and then take it with vengeance.

She turned back to the QB and asked, "So do you need an audience or is he jealous because you get to put your hands in his crouch?" The QB chuckled then looked behind her and said, "Pull the curtain and go watch the door." Liz heard the boy leave and the curtain pulled, she then saw a stool a couple of feet to her left, so she stepped over dropped her books onto it, and stepped back. Liz had spent four months training and preparing herself for this event. She readied her mind and then stepped forward closer to the boy. Visions of Jimmy Dittle invaded her thoughts as she looked at the QB. She remembered her father saying, "Don't think about what they did to you, think about what you will do to them."

The QB took a couple of steps forward as Liz pushed her hands into her back pockets. He watched the expression on her face as he reached out with his right hand to caress her cheek. Liz showed no emotion and kept watching the QB. The QB then let his right-hand slide down and his fingers pressed against her left breast. Liz didn't withdraw or show any emotion but watched as a smile crept across his face.

Liz shook her head and said, "Boys, don't you know how to touch a woman?" The QB smirked and retorted, "I thought I was?" Liz shook her head again, slowly brought her hands from her rear pockets, and then gently placed her right hand over his right hand so her fingers could curl under the heel of his hand. She then moved her left hand over her right hand and pressed the QB's hand harder onto her breast. The smile on the QB's face grew.

Liz took another step forward and moved to her left just a smidge to get the proper angle as a sly smile crept across her face. She had the QB exactly where she wanted him, this was her window, and she was going to take it with vengeance.

The QB then used his fingers to press against her breast more, and his smile grew. Liz then said, "Look when a woman allows you to touch her, she wants you to claim her, take her like she is yours." Liz then pressed his hands harder into her breast until he couldn't move his finger at all. The QB said, "You're pressing too hard." Liz's smile grew and replied, "Oh really?"

Liz then moved her right foot back just a few inches and then shoved her left shoulder forward and down while holding his hand firmly against her breast. This forced his arm to bend backward in a manner it wasn't supposed to as she strained his elbow and the ligaments of his arm almost to the breaking point. The QB had to drop onto his knees on the floor and use his left hand to support himself and prevent his elbow from shattering. Liz then used her grip on the heel of his hand to peel it off her breast and stepped back pinning his little finger back. If he tried to rise, it would cause his finger or elbow to break.

Liz could see Jimmy Dittle on the floor before her when she took a step back and delivered two roundhouse kicks to his face. Liz twisted the QB's arm some more, he gave out a yelp of pain; she then delivered two more frontal kicks of her boot heel, into his face.

The Center finally reacted to the QB's cry of pain, and wrapping his arm around Liz, he picked her up and moved back away from the QB who was still on his hands and knees on the floor. The Center placed her on the floor and then called over asking, "Dude, you, okay?"

Liz looked down to see where his feet were, she saw he was wearing sandals, she then stood up straight and pushed her arms up so he would press down, she then raised her right leg and drove her heel down hard onto the top of his right foot. The force of her blow broke the Metatarsal bone in his foot and caused the Center to give out a cry of pain and loosened his grip a little but not enough. Liz then moved her hips to the right, raised her left fist, and delivered a hammer blow into his groin, and this time his grip left as he grabbed his groin, and stumbled back.

Liz then delivered a left elbow to his nose, which caused him to stand back up. Liz followed this with a kick to the inside of his right knee with her right heel and he collapsed onto his knees. Liz spun and delivered a roundhouse kick to the side of his head, and he was out cold. The entire confrontation only took a few seconds. Liz suddenly felt empowered, strong, and dangerous. She had never felt like this before, she liked it.

Liz now turned her attention back to the QB who was still on his knees but had risen straight with blood running down his face. He had vicious gashes on his cheek, his nose was tilted to one side and his left eye was closed, there was blood on his jersey and jeans.

As Liz slowly approached, she fixed her eyes on his and said, "When a woman doesn't want you to touch her, then you deserve whatever she does to you." With that, she took a small hop, and she delivered a hard roundhouse kick into his face breaking his jaw and sending him over backwards onto his back out cold.

Liz found a rag and cleaned the blood off her boots; she then checked herself and found a little blood on her sleeve and the toe of her other boot. She tried to clean them, then picked up her books, and exited the rear of the theater, and crossed the hall into the classroom. The teacher stood up and looked angrily at Liz demanding, "You're late . . . do you have a pass?" Liz was walking to her desk in the rear of the room and as she sat down, she replied, "No I don't, I left it with the boys across the hall."

The teacher's eyes grew large as she looked around the room and ordered, "Everyone remain in your seats, I will be right back." The teacher exited the room. Students having sex in the back of the theater had become a problem and she had to investigate. Liz opened her book and began to read the assigned chapter, but she found it hard to concentrate.

The girl next to her touched her arm and asked what was happening but Liz just shook her head then said, "I think someone got hurt." She didn't want to confess to anything. After about ten minutes, the door opened and the principal appeared, he was looking directly at Liz.

Liz and the Principal locked gazes then he raised his hand and with one finger signaled for her to come. Liz closed her books and walked to the principal then followed him to his office. They passed the medics pushing a gurney out the backdoor of the theater, when they entered his office, the principal motioned for her to sit in front of his desk as he walked around and sat behind it. Liz held her books to her chest and watched as he straightened some papers then slid them to one side.

The principal then looked intently at Liz and asked, "Can you explain what happened?" Liz shrugged her shoulders and replied, "The QB wanted to talk to me." The principal nodded sullenly then asked, "What about?" Liz studied him closely and replied, "Sir it was a private conversation, and I can't talk about it without his permission." The principal looked shocked at the answer but then nodded and countered, "Well the QB isn't talking much; his jaw is broken, along with his cheekbone and nose. As for the other young man, his knee is dislocated and his jaw and foot both have broken bones too."

Liz gave a raised eyebrow at the news but nothing else. The principal nodded then placed both hands palm down on his desk and asked, "You were alone with those two?" Liz nodded yes so, the principal asked, "Are you sure you didn't see anyone else; did you see Mathew Chambers anywhere?" Liz shook her head no, and then the principal nodded and said, "I called your home, and someone is on the way, we can sit and talk until they arrive." The principal then leaned back and asked, "You have changed a lot, I understand your mother was married this summer?" Liz gave a smile and nodded, not saying anything.

The principal then asked, "You look a little more in shape this year, have you been exercising this summer?" Liz smiled and shrugged her shoulders. The principal looked around his desk then back at Liz and asked, "So where did your parents go for their honeymoon?" Liz smiled and replied, "We went to his vacation home." The principal nodded as he studied Liz; she had answered his questions but gave him nothing.

The principal continued to make small talk to learn anything, but Liz continued to give him nothing. Ten minutes later, there was a knock on the door and the principal commanded, "Enter." Samantha came in, sat down beside Liz, and asked, "Are you okay darling?" Liz nodded yes and glanced at the principal. Sam looked at the principal and asked, "Can I have a word with my daughter alone?" The principal nodded then exited and closed the door; Sam turned back to Liz and nodded.

Liz took a deep breath and started speaking quickly, "The Center grabbed me and dragged me into the back of the Theater for the QB, and I decided to kick their asses." Sam smiled and replied, "They didn't hurt you, did they?" Liz smiled and shook her head no.

Sam then asked, "So how do you feel about all the sweating and training you had to endure this summer?" Liz looked down then back up into her mother's face, and smiled then replied, "I wasn't scared, Jamie and Susan had been preaching to me to watch, evaluate, then wait for the opening, I didn't think about what they wanted to do to me, I kept thinking about what I was going to do to them."

Sam smiled then looked back at the principal and motioned for him to come back. When the Principal sat down Sam asked, "Where were the boys found?" The principal looked intently at Samantha and answered, "In the back of the theater." Sam nodded and asked, "So they dragged my little girl into the back of the theater where no one could see them, she could have been rapped, and that door isn't locked, why?"

The principal adjusted in his seat and then replied, "We can't lock the door for security reasons." Sam then demanded, "Of course, if it was locked the boys who drag young girls into the back of the theater wouldn't be secure in their privacy as they rap them, and we can't have that can we?"

The principal's eyes grew large, and his face went pale then he shook his head saying, "Ms. Raven, that is not why we leave it unlocked . . . "Sam then stood and proclaimed, "Well I think those boys got what they deserved." Sam then looked at Liz and asked, "You want to stay or go home?" Liz smiled and replied, "I'm fine Mom."

Sam looked back at the principal and demanded, "I expect her safety to be your utmost concern." She then looked at Liz and said, 'I'm only allowing you to stay because that is what you want, but if I hear of anything else happening, I will return with my lawyer."

The principal nodded furiously and stammered, "I will make sure your daughter is looked after, please accept my apology." Sam motioned for Liz to come with her and as they left the office she whispered, "Matt will hear of this and be upset." Liz smiled and replied, "I'll take care of him, don't worry."

CHAPTER 28:
The game that changed everything

At lunch, Liz explained to Matt what had happened." The principal didn't think their families would sue. How were they going to explain how a five-foot little girl of just over one hundred pounds could take out two, six-foot football players?"

Matt was upset. "Is your mother going to tell Trevor?" Liz shook her head. Matt was worried that Trevor would fire him for not protecting her, but he wanted to reassure Liz. "I told you that you could do it."

Later that afternoon, the football team found out that the backup QB and center would take over since there was no way the other players would be playing. It immediately became apparent that the new QB would be recruited from the junior varsity team. He was shorter, but he was also quicker and more accurate. Those facts didn't make the players feel better, but they were both fresh off the JV team. Could they hack it on varsity?

That Friday, they faced Gainesville, one of the most proficient teams in Georgia high school football. They hadn't lost a game in two years, and they were blowing everyone out. The offensive coordinator asked to use Matt as a tight end to simulate Gainesville's tight end. This adjustment gave Matt experience at catching the ball in coverage and running routes. On Friday night, Trevor, Sam, and Liz along with Jamie and Susan were in the stands to watch the game. Winder dropped to a twenty-four-point underdog, and everyone understood that there was no way they could win.

Gainesville won the toss and chose to receive the ball. They got the ball on their twenty-five. Gainesville couldn't move the ball, so they punted. The Winder return man caught the punt but fumbled it on Winder's thirty, and a Gainesville player picked it up and scampered thirty yards for a touchdown.

Gainesville kicked off, but this time, the Winder return man carried the ball to the forty-five. Winder was able to move the ball to the Gainesville twenty-five, where the running back fumbled, and Gainesville took it over. Gainesville couldn't move the ball on the first two plays then on third and fifteen they threw a deep pass, which was almost intercepted by the Winder cornerback, but the ball bounced off his hands and the Gainesville receiver caught it and went fifty yards for a second touchdown.

Gainesville kicked off again, and Winder returned it to the thirty. However, two offsides and a holding play forced them back to the ten-yard line when they attempted to punt, it was blocked for a third touchdown! They had just started the second quarter, and Gainesville was up twenty-one points. When Gainesville kicked off again, Winder returned it to the thirty-five and pushed Gainesville to the twenty, where they attempted a field goal…they missed. Nothing seemed to be going right for Winder.

Trevor, Sam, Jamie, Susan, and Liz were all in the stands watching the game, and Winder was losing on account of their own mistakes. Liz looked at her father. "It doesn't look good, does it?"

Trevor nodded. "Well, if Gainesville can score twenty-one points in a half, Winder can do the same."

The two teams retired to their locker rooms, and the Winder coaches talked to their squads, trying to analyze what went wrong and get them back into the game. The Winder players were nervous and intimidated…they weren't playing their best game. They were whining and fretting about what the second half would bring.

The normally quiet and calm Mathew was sitting at his locker fuming as he watched and listened to his teammates lament how they were being killed. Gainesville averaged forty points per game, and they already had twenty-one. They were too good for Winder to beat them.

The team was demoralized and ready to give up, when Matt stood up, slammed his helmet into the locker, walked to the center of the locker room, and yelled, "What's wrong with you guys?! They can't move against us, and if it weren't for the mistakes we made, they wouldn't be on the scoreboard. We have put three long drives together, and if everyone does their job, we can beat them."

Matt stopped and looked at each young man. "We are down 21 points; we weren't supposed to win anyway, so what the hell have we got to lose? I'm going out on that field. I'm going to play and show them that I will not be defeated. Those of you who don't believe we can win can get the hell out. Those of you, who want to win, come with me." Matt snatched up his helmet and walked out of the locker room.

The entire locker room fell silent. They had never seen Matt give an outburst like that, and it shocked them. They all looked at each other, and the entire team jumped up and ran out onto the field. The coaches looked at each other in shock and followed.

Winder got the ball to start the second half, and the return man took it out to the thirty-five. The QB scrambled and threw short passes to advance down to the Gainesville forty-five when Winder pulled a draw play where the QB pretended to scramble but handed it off to the speedy full-back who then rambled twenty yards to the Gainesville twenty-five. Gainesville's defense was excellent---they had only allowed 10 points in the two previous games with four shutouts last season.

Gainesville's defense stiffened and Winder had to settle for a field goal. They were on the board but were still losing 21 to 3. By Winder scoring, they proved to themselves that they were up to the challenge, and maybe Mathew was right. This realization fueled the players, and for the first time, they believed that their first two wins weren't by luck, but because they were better. Their expression changed; their attitude changed; and their play changed.

Winder kicked off, and the kicker sent the ball through the end zone. It was something he could do in practice, but so far, this was the first time during a game. This maneuver gave Gainesville the ball on the 20. Gainesville wanted to send a message, and the first play involved their two-hundred-forty-pound fullback in a dive play off the right guard. Matt took a step back--- he was thinking of a pass, but then he saw the linemen cross-block and open a hole. The Gainesville fullback was famous for running over people and was ready to punish Winder.

Matt charged into the hole and met the fullback head-on. The force of his blow stopped the fullback cold. Matt forced him back into the backfield and threw him down. Matt stood up and looked down at the shocked fullback. His team yelled, "Yeah! That's how it is done!"

This sent a chill through everyone watching: the coaches, the teams, and the bleachers on both sides. All stood up in shock. No one had been able to stop the fullback until that play. Matt trotted back into the defense huddle yelling and encouraging his team.

The next play was a pass to the right, and again, the receiver was dropped for no gain. On third and ten, they attempted a double-reverse handoff, which only got them five yards because Matt ran down the halfback and tackled him. Gainesville had to punt. It seemed that the Winder players were suddenly faster, stronger, and now dominating the Gainesville players.

Winder received the ball on the thirty, and the shifty returner carried it back to the forty-five. Again, the QB used his speed and elusiveness to evade the Gainesville blitz and connect for short gains to begin advancing the ball.

Gainesville was using man-to-man coverage, but no defensive corner can cover for long. Soon the receiver would get loose, and that was when the Winder QB would hit him. He was carving up the Gainesville defense like a Thanksgiving turkey. He was moving the ball, and when they committed seven men to cover the receivers, he handed off to the running back, who gained another ten yards. It took six plays, but Winder pushed the ball to the Gainesville fifteen when the QB threw a flair pass to the tight end. That gained five yards, but he was hit hard by the linebacker and hurt.

Matt had been standing behind the head coach and his two assistants when he saw their only tight end helped off the field. He stepped forward and touched the defense coach. "I can go in as the tight end."

The defensive coach looked at him seriously. "Are you sure?"

Matt gave him a determined look. "Hell yeah! Put me in." The defense coach leaned over and spoke to the head coach, who then looked back at Matt and nodded. Matt pushed out and headed onto the field.

Winder huddled up and when Matt appeared in the huddle. The QB gave a big smile and called a sweep around his end. Matt lined up on the right side, and they brought in the second-string tackle to line up in the backfield. When the QB received the ball, he tossed it to the running back, who started toward the right side. Matt fired off into the defensive end, forcing him back, and peeled off to hinder the center linebacker following the play. The two receivers blocked the corner and safety, and the second-string tackle took out the second safety as the running back scooted ten yards into the end zone for a touchdown. Winder was now trailing 21 to 10.

Winder kicked off again, and once more, it was a touchback. Gainesville started on their twenty-yard line and got one first down before they stalled again and had to punt. This time, the Winder receiver caught the ball on Winder's fifteen and got to the twenty before he was tackled. The Winder offense started to move the ball by using the QB's quickness and throwing skills to shred the Gainesville defense.

The Gainesville defense had been on the field for most of the second and third quarters, and man-to-man coverage required the defensive backs to follow the receiver wherever they went. This tactic wore out the defensive back quickly; it was now late in the third quarter, and they were exhausted. Gainesville had to substitute the first-string players for younger players who of course were not as good. This helped the Winder receivers.

The Winder QB went into shotgun formation with Matt on the right and two receivers to his right. The receivers took off at lightning speed and then slanted to the center of the field, pulling the coverage with them so Matt hit the defensive end. He peeled off into the open flat towards the sideline. The QB sidestepped the blitz and then hit Matt in full stride before taking off down the right side of the field. The linebacker underestimated Matt's speed, so he missed Matt, and he crossed the fifty before being forced out of bounds on the Gainesville forty. The third quarter ended.

In the next play, they brought their fastest wideout who took a step inward and took off down the left side. He quickly outpaced the tiring defender, and the Winder QB hit him in full stride for another thirty-yard gain to the Gainesville ten. During the next play, Matt pushed past the defensive end and ran along the five-yard line toward the center of the field. The QB noticed the center linebacker blitz and ducked out of the way. He leaped forward and hit Matt as he came open.

Matt caught the ball and pushed forward to the two-yard line, where they finally wrestled him down. Winder then called a draw, and the running back scored their second touchdown. The score was now 21 to 17.

Gainesville was able to return the kickoff to their thirty, and they pushed the ball to their forty. Again, they stalled and had to punt. This time, Winder fielded the ball on their own ten and advanced to fifteen with less than seven minutes to play. Gainesville was now playing for their lives, but their defense was worn out. They tried switching the coverage to zone, hoping that they could pull an interception. Winder accelerated their offense so Gainesville couldn't substitute.

The Winder QB recognized the change and told his receiver that he would pick a different receiver during each down to just find an open spot downfield and stay there---the rest would remain running. The QB was hitting them for five to fifteen yards, and Gainesville was unable to stop him.

They couldn't figure out whom to double-team because he kept hitting different receivers. American football is not like any other sport. American football is like war. Two teams are assembled with all types of people. Big ones who play linemen and their job is to push people around. Smaller ones who are running backs who carry the ball. Then the tall thin players are the wide receivers. Unlike many other sports American Football uses players of all sizes, strengths, and abilities.

Each Coach knows the weaknesses and strengths of his team and his job is to put together a plan that will help his team and nullify the assets of the opposing team. It's two armies coming together, and the emotion and effort are like being on a battlefield, only no lives are lost. On this night these two armies met and while the stronger team dominated the first half, the weaker team found their strength and were now fighting back.

Winder was the underdog and had trailed all game and after forty-five minutes of fighting it had now come to less than 10 minutes of play. Could the undefeated champions who hadn't lost a game in two years stop this underdog team who weren't even supposed to be in this game, from winning?

The parents and friends of the players of both teams had their hearts in their throats, hoping beyond hope, that their team would prevail. This is the story of every American football game and why the people of America so love it. Any team can beat any other team if they only have the desire to win.

CHAPTER 29:
Win some lose some

Winder again began moving the ball, but Gainesville knew now that they had to stop them or lose the game. Gainesville hadn't lost a game in two years, and they didn't want some upstart loser like Winder to defeat them.

The Winder QB started again with quick passes. They had scrambled two plays for a first down. On first down at Winder's forty-two, the QB again showed pass. The coverage fell back, rushing four. The QB took off running and slid down on Gainesville's thirty-yard line. During the next play, Matt was again the right tight end with receivers on both sides. The receivers went down and out while Matt ran straight down the center of the field. He was wide open and got fifteen yards. When the Winder QB hit him, he went another five yards before the safeties were able to stop him on Gainesville fifteen.

The next ten yards were torturous, and it took three plays to get the ball onto the five-yard line for another first down. Only ninety seconds of playing time remained. During the first play, they tried their previous sweep play, but it only gained three yards. The second play was a draw for another yard. It was now third and one with only twenty seconds left to play.

The third down was a QB sneak, which gained zilch. It was now fourth and one with the game on the line. This time, Matt lined up on the left with the same tackle as halfback. Instead of handing off to the running back, the QB followed his backs around the left side as Matt and the receivers collided with defensive players. A pile of bodies collected on the goal line as Gainesville fought to stop them. Winder was determined to score. It was a battle of wills, but the QB was able to squeeze between Matt and the second-string tackle.

The QB could only get so far, he felt the tackle reach back and grab his belt, then Matt reached back and grabbed his belt, and they pushed the QB into the end zone for the final score. The cheers and groans rose as the pile of humanity landed in the end zone.

After the extra point, everyone realized that Winder had scored twenty-four points during the second half while holding Gainesville's potent offense to only one hundred yards throughout the entire game. They had accomplished the impossible. They had beaten Gainesville.

This game marked a turning point for the Winder football team and for Mathew Chambers. The once quiet and shy young man had blossomed into a force to be reckoned with, and Winder football was now on a winning streak. Every opposing team would watch and keep note of Mathew.

Winder's next 7 games were routes. They averaged forty points per game while only allowing 28 in all 7 games. No defense could stop them, and no team could move consistently against them. They were now coming down to the last game of the season: homecoming.

On Tuesday, Liz was closing her locker when a tall blonde slammed her hand against the locker. "Who do you think you are putting your name in for homecoming queen?!"

Liz looked up at her in surprise. "I have no idea what you are talking about . . . I have no desire to be homecoming queen."

The tall blonde stood up straight and crossed her arms over her chest. "Then you won't mind when I win?"

Liz was about to say something when Matt appeared and pulled Liz around to face him. "Guess what the guys did? They put your name in for homecoming queen!"

Liz gave Matt a shocked look and angrily replied, "What! Why did you do that!?"

The tall blonde overheard Matt and interjected, "It won't matter... I'm going to win anyway." She marched off down the hall with her minions in tow.

Matt rolled his eyes. "Don't worry about her. One of the guys said that you should run, and all the other guys got excited about it."

Liz shook her head and stepped toward Matt angrily. "You know Daddy doesn't like publicity, and this isn't going to make him happy." Matt suddenly realized that this might not have been a good idea.

Liz pinched Matt's arm. "Go back and take my name off that list."

Matt was wide-eyed. "Okay, but all the guys said they would love to vote for you after what you did. I'm sure we can get them to vote for the other bimbo rather than that snob."

Liz gave Matt a serious look and retorted, "You'd better."

On Thursday, Trevor was sitting in his office reading a newspaper when Mathew and Elizabeth came into the office. Trevor saw immediately that Liz looked very upset, and Matt looked like he had to put on chainmail shorts to protect his butt from the ass-chewing he just received. Trevor motioned for them to sit in the two chairs in front of his desk. Liz turned away from Matt and crossed her arms and legs. Matt glanced at Liz and turned to face Trevor. "You wanted to see us, sir?"

Trevor picked up the newspaper lying on his desk and held it up so Liz and Matt could see it. "Can either of you explain this picture or the article about Liz in the paper?"

Liz glared at Matt, and he flinched as if she was going to hit him again. "Yeah, Matt. Please explain how after I told you to not vote for me... AND EVERYONE DID!?"

Matt fletched every time Liz waved her hands around. "When Cliff said you should run and then all the guys on the team said yeah, I thought you would be happy to know how much everyone in the school looks up to you even though... you're shorter than everyone else."

Liz stood up and faced Matt with her arms crossed and one foot forward slightly with her toe-tapping. Trevor had seen that stance before from her mother and had to cover his mouth with his hand to hide the snicker on his face. Liz was looking down at Matt now. "I told you Dad wouldn't like it, and you promised to get them to vote for the bimbo." At that, a voice from the office door sang out, "Congratulations honey! I hear you're the new homecoming queen."

Everyone looked up at Samantha walking across the office towards Trevor. Sam was now seven months pregnant and showing. As she walked, she held her belly. Liz looked at her mother. "Don't blame me, Mom. I didn't put my name in---Matt did." As Sam passed Liz, she patted the chair. Liz sat back down but turned away from Matt.

Sam walked around the desk and stood next to Trevor. She looked at Matt. "Matt, you asked your friends to vote for the bimbo?"

Matt nodded. "There's this snob named Sue Anne and she is stuck-up. She was expecting to win. Her only competition was Mary Lou, another bimbo, and I asked everyone to vote for her."

Sam looked seriously at Matt. "So, you did ask them to vote for the bimbo?"

Liz turned to Mathew. "Results show they did!"

Sam looked intently at Matt. "Did they?"

Matt looked at Liz and then back at Sam. "No, no I asked them to vote for the other bimbo, not this one...I mean not Liz. But once everyone saw her name on the ballot, they all wanted to vote for her. We even made-up new ballots without her name on it, and they wrote her in."

Liz turned and looked at Matt angrily. "If you had never started that nonsense with me on the ballot, they never would have voted for me."

Matt twisted in his seat and pleaded with Liz. "No Liz, I had little to do with it. They just asked me if you would like it. I said you would be honored, but I didn't put your name on the ballot. Elizabeth, you must understand how much everyone respects you for taking out those two football players."

Trevor sat up straight and demanded, "Excuse me, what football players?"

Liz looked over at Trevor with a shy grin and shrugged her shoulders. "The QB and his center dragged me into the back of the theater and tried to rape me. I took them out."

Matt looked at Trevor and said, "It was great, sir. He wasn't a good QB, and he was a dick. When Liz kicked his ass, the entire school cheered."

Trevor looked at Sam. "What's wrong honey---hate playing catch up?" Trevor shook his head at his beautiful wife with her sly smile and he knew she had this one.

He gave a sour look and looked back at Matt. "So, what was the count?"

Matt finally had something good. He stood up and proclaimed, "It was a landslide, sir. I don't think either of the bimbos got more than thirty votes."

Trevor glanced at his lovely wife then back at Matt and Liz. "Well, congratulations dear . . . You just won the homecoming queen. I read the article, and they used an old picture. It was superficial at best and gave your address as Winder. Go to the dance; enjoy yourself, then dinner and straight home." Trevor gave Matt a serious look. "Correct?" Matt enthusiastically nodded in agreement.

Trevor opened the drawer of his desk, removed a silver box, and motioned for Liz to approach. "This is for you."

Liz opened the box to find a silver and diamond watch. Liz's eyes grew large, and a big smile spread over her face. "I thought you were mad at me?"

Trevor glanced at Matt. "I am because you didn't tell me about those two football players, but I still love you---that won't change." Matt and Liz exited the office, and Sam turned to lean against the desk with her hand on her swollen belly. Trevor put his hand on hers and his ear to her belly. He looked up into Sam's face and smiled.

Sam asked, "Do you think that watch will be enough?"

Trevor looked seriously at Sam. "I hope so. She isn't quite as easy to bug as you were." They both chuckled.

CHAPTER 30:
Home Coming queen and a big surprise

The homecoming game was against a good team, but Winder was on a roll. By the third quarter, the game was well in hand, despite the other team pulling every trick-play in the book. Matt ended with several tackles for losses and two interceptions, one for a touchdown. Because homecoming also included a meet-and-greet of all the football players at the high school. The actual festival and dance occurred on Saturday afternoon and night. After the festival, Trevor and Liz returned to the plantation to get dressed for the dance.

Matt's parents came to the Plantation, and Matt arrived in the foyer dressed in a rented tuxedo. The doors to the elevator opened, and Samantha and Elizabeth exited into the foyer. Matt stood beside his parents when she walked out dressed in a Susie Wong White silk gown that was shallow in the front but bare down the back and slit cut up the side almost to her hips. She wore a black pearl necklace and earrings with black, high-heeled shoes and her new watch. The white gown and accessories highlighted her hair and beauty. She was a vision!

When Matt saw her, he forgot how to breathe. His eyes grew large as he watched her float across the room towards him. She spoke, but Matt couldn't hear---he was transfixed by her beauty, and he couldn't believe she was with him.

Liz walked to Mathew and asked," You look nice. Are you ready to go?" She looked up into his face and realized he hadn't heard her, so she patted him on the chest. Matt blinked, took a deep breath, and nodded. Liz smiled as she looked up into his face with a sly smile. "Forget to breathe?"

Matt blinked again and mumbled, "Ah yeah, I think so?"

Matt held up the corsage and handed it to Liz. She smiled as he slipped it onto her wrist, covering her watch. They posed for pictures and climbed into Matt's truck which had been cleaned and polished just for this date. At nine-thirty, they announced the queen and king of the dance, and Liz went up on stage to receive her crown. Afterward, Liz and Matt danced until ten and drove to Ruby Tuesdays in downtown Winder for dinner. They also visited Fargo State Park and parked, overlooking the lake.

Matt undid his seatbelt and then looked at Liz. Liz gave Matt a seductive look, then slid over to sit in his lap and give him a long, passionate kiss. As they kissed, a car drove up behind them. The lights on top of the car flooded Matt's truck, and two officers walked up to the driver's side, tapping on the window. Matt helped Liz slide back to her side of the truck and he lowered his window a little. "Can I help you, officers?"

"Please step out of the vehicle, sir."

Matt glanced over at Liz and rolled the window down a little further. "Officers, we are not doing anything wrong." The officers glanced at each other and repeated the order, but with more force. Matt nodded and started to push the door open when one officer grabbed the door and forced it open. The other officer reached in and pulled him out, slamming him into the side of the truck. They started punching and kicking him until he was bloodied, bruised, and unconscious.

Liz started screaming as she saw Matt being attacked. As one officer reached into the truck for her, she shrunk back to the other door. It suddenly opened, and she was dragged out, kicking, and screaming. They pushed her against the truck so they could handcuff her then tossed her into the back of the car and quickly pulled out. Liz had lost her shoes, but slowly she sat up in the back seat and looked at the two men in the front seat. She surveyed the vehicle and saw the radios and computers. At first, she was scared, but then her fear instinctually turned to fury. "Do you pigs realize how much trouble you're in?"

Back at the Plantation, an alarm was being sent to all the cell phones, and people came charging into the control room. Trevor arrived first, and then Jamie and Susan arrived together. Right behind them was Jeff and finally, Sam. Trevor walked in and asked, "What's up?"

Gary glanced over his shoulder as they entered. "What you predicted has happened."

Trevor nodded. "Show us the video."

Sam had just arrived when Gary moved the two videos from inside the truck cab onto the sixty-inch screen. They watched what had happened inside of the truck. They couldn't see what was happening outside of the truck, but from the way Liz was screaming and the shaking of the cameras, it was obvious. Then they saw Liz being pulled out of the truck then soon after the other vehicle departed.

Trevor looked at Gary. "You got a bead on that car?"

Gary brought four more windows with videos. "Not yet, but I will say this, they looked like they were police. I'm trying to get a license on the vehicle."

Sam was watching the screen. "You put cameras inside the truck?"

Trevor glanced at Gary who immediately turned away. Trevor quietly said, "Can we talk about this later?"

Jamie asked, "Gary didn't the rear camera pickup something when they pulled up?"

Sam looked up at Trevor again. "How many cameras did you put onto that truck?"

Trevor looked back at Jamie then at Sam and whispered, "Six, but can we talk about this later?"

Sam gave him a harder look but let it go. Jamie and Susan glanced at each other, and Susan said, "We need to get ready."

They took off, and Trevor asked, "You still tracking her?"

Gary nodded. "I got her. Go get ready."

Trevor turned to Jeff. "You'd better get ready too."

Five minutes later, Trevor walked out to the black SUV parked in front of the mansion as Jamie was pushing her AR-15 with infrared scope along with another bag into the back. Jamie and Susan were all dressed in black with combat boots and tactical gloves, armed with silenced pistols and knives. Trevor was also clad in black with a 511 tactical jacket and a pistol hidden in the linings. Jeff soon appeared dressed just like the others. As they were placing their gear in the vehicle, Sam walked to Trevor and said, "You be careful, but bring our baby girl back." Trevor kissed her and climbed into the back seat.

As the vehicle pulled out Trevor called Gary. "What's the status?"

Gary clicked some keys and replied, "Start to Athens, and I will send the GPS to your vehicle."

Trevor disconnected and ordered, "Head to Athens, and bring up the GPS. Jeff, get the com gear out. We need to check it." Jeff reached into the back, pulled the bag over, and removed some items. Suddenly, the GPS screen flickered, and a red dot indicated Trevor's crew appeared.

Another dot appeared, but this one was blue, and it wasn't stationary. Susan was driving and glanced at the screen then at Jamie, who looked over her shoulder, at Trevor. They saw where the blue dot was. It was just inside the city limits of Athens. They knew what it meant. Trevor asked, "How long until we arrive?"

Jamie reported to Trevor, "Ten minutes out, sir." Trevor sat back and attached one of the COM devices to his belt. He put the earpiece in his ear.

The police vehicle turned right down an industrial road and then left in between two warehouses. They then drove a third of the way down and turned left past a door that had just opened into the first warehouse. Once they parked the vehicle, they had to fight to get Liz out, but they finally extricated Liz from the back seat. One officer threw her over his shoulder and carried her up a set of stairs to a large room.

The room was dark. She couldn't see a thing except for a single chair under the only ceiling light in the room. The two officers dragged her in, and duct-taped her to the chair with her hands still cuffed behind her. They retreated into the darkness like vermin. Liz looked around for something, anything, but nothing was visible.

Liz heard a door open, and it squeaked when it closed. She tried to make out where the sound was coming from, but it was echoing from everywhere. A light came on about thirty feet to her right and there was someone in a wheelchair beneath the light. Whoever was in the chair was leaning forward so she couldn't see them.

The person moved out of the light and when it stopped; another light came on above him. Liz sat back, looked at the person curiously, and thought, "Talk about being melodramatic!" The person advanced again and again until the light was directly above him. Liz looked focused again on the wheelchair and decided if they wanted to kill her, she would be dead. They were wasting time, and she knew Trevor would arrive soon.

The wheelchair person made the final move and arrived just six feet in front of her, when the light illuminated it revealed him. The person sat up straight and looked dead into her eyes. Liz's nightmares bled into her reality.

It was Jimmy Dittle.

CHAPTER 31:
Clearing things up

Sam watched them leave and the worry for everyone came over her in waves. She didn't want anyone hurt but this was the second time her daughter had been kidnapped and it made her angry. If she weren't pregnant, she would have demanded to go as well. Her one consoling fact was that Trevor had his crew, and they were on the road within minutes after it occurred. She didn't have to wait five days to find out the outcome. Sam knew Trevor would bring Liz back. She then decided she needed to talk to Gary.

Gary just got off the phone with security requesting they send two men to retrieve Matt and his truck from Fargo Lake Park. He found the GPS of the Truck then gave them the coordinates of the truck so they could locate it quickly and hung up the phone. He was typing when he felt the hair on the back of his neck rise. He carefully peeked over his left shoulder to see Sam standing behind him then quickly hunched over as if he was extremely busy and found the plans for the two buildings where the crew was heading.

It was then he felt the hand on his shoulder as Sam said, "You can stop pretending Gary, you are going to tell me about those cameras."

Gary gave a glance and in a pleading voice, "A what cameras maim?"

Sam sent her fingers into the nerve in his shoulder and pulled him back then leaned over into his face as she said, "Do you want me to tell Jamie that you just lied to me, Gary, I like you but you better start talking right now! And don't call me Maim!"

Gary gave a wince then nodded and pointed to the computer to his left then slowly moved to the computer and clicked on a shortcut that took them to a folder where there were more than a dozen videos. Sam asked, "Did you call security to go get Matt?" Gary had turned back to his computer and nodded then said, "Yes maim." Sam hit him on the back. Gary responded with, "I mean Mrs. Paterson."

Sam began going through the videos and realized there were six cameras on the truck Matt had been driving. Four were on the outside looking in four directions but two were inside the cab. They appeared to be in the windshield column, and each was looking across the cab to the other side. The first half dozen was Liz kissing Matt. Matt never made the first move, it was always Liz, and it appeared that Matt was holding back as if he was afraid to touch Liz.

Then Sam found the video of Matt working on the fence and Liz was helping him. She checked the date, and it was the Saturday after their game with Gainesville. Liz was wearing her Daisy Duke shorts, and her hair was in two ponytails. She struggled with the branches to pull them back away from the fence. It looked like they were having fun.

Sam remembered that day because Liz wanted to go and work with Matt on the fence. It was the first time she had asked. She helped Liz pack lunch in a picnic basket for Liz to take. Sam was shocked when Liz suddenly pulled a bottle of wine from the basket and handed it to Mathew.

A small smile crossed Sam's lips as she shook her head and whispered, "I didn't give you that little girl, what are you planning to do?" Sam glanced at Gary and then stopped the video, she smacked Gary on his back and demanded, "Gary who has seen this video?" Gary meekly turned to Sam and looked at the screen and his face went white as he pushed away from Sam and quietly said, "Me, maim, I'm the only one who has seen any of those videos." Sam wheeled closer to him and demanded, "Gary if you are lying to me, I will have Jamie castrate you, has anyone else seen then."

Gary held both hands up and begged, "Please Mrs. Paterson, I haven't shown them to anyone, honest." Sam went back to the video and watched as Liz spread out a blanket behind the truck in perfect view of the camera. They sat and drank, ate, and laughed, and then Liz leaned into Matt and kissed him. Liz then straddled Matt's lap, pulled the hem of his t-shirt up over his head, and pulled it off. Sam was thinking, yeah girl he looks good without his shirt, as she smiled.

Then Liz pushed him back onto the ground and was on top of Matt kissing suddenly she was pushing something down then she stood up with the bottom of Matt's trousers and pulled them off. Matt only had his underwear on now.

Sam watched in horror as Liz was now standing over Matt looking down at him with her back to the camera and pulling her top off. Sam's hand went to her mouth to quiet the gasp as Liz then removed her shorts. Before Liz tossed her shorts aside, she removed something from the back pocket. Liz was now naked as she lowered herself down onto Matt. Matt was sitting up and shaking his head no, but it didn't appear that Liz was listening, and she was nodding yes.

She watched as Liz pushed Matt back down onto the ground as if he had no strength. Sam was thinking this man could press two hundred pounds and this one-hundred-pound girl was pushing him around as if he was as weak as a kitten. Sam knew what Liz was doing, she was claiming her man, and she was in complete control. She watched as Liz kissed Matt and then made love to him right there in front of the camera.

It was a very romantic video, except for the fact that she was watching her daughter having sex with Liz's boyfriend. Sam sat back reached over and hit Gary on the back again then demanded, "How many are like this one?" Gary glanced back and said, "There are two more good ones I mean bad ones, where Liz went into the woods with Matt and . . . did . . . what they did." Sam nodded then asked, "How many did you watch?" Gary's face turned red then purple looked down then back and said, "I only watched the first one, honest, the other I fast-forwarded through them." Sam gave him an intense glare then said, "Liar, put these on a DVD and give it to me, then erase all of them, if you get anymore, I want them, understand?" Gary nodded quickly.

When they found Matt and his truck the two men ran to Matt as he was trying to get up, he was on his knees when they got to him with both doors to the truck open. Matt looked up at the man then around then in horror he hollered, "Where is she, where is Liz, Oh My God! They took her, they took her!"

The men helped Matt up and guided him to their SUV as Matt protested saying, "We have to go after her, Call Trevor, we need to get her back." The men pushed Matt into the SUV and said, "We already have a crew heading after them, we're taking you to the mansion."

As they buckled Matt into the SUV, the two security men then jumped into the vehicles and pulled out heading back to the plantation. When they arrived at the mansion, Sam was at the door to greet them. Matt was visibly upset that he had lost Liz. Matt looked at Sam with tears in his eyes then he said, "They took her, they took her, I couldn't stop them."

Sam guided them to the elevator so they could get Matt to the medical center in the basement. Sam stayed with Matt until the Med Tech arrived then went back to the control room and finished watching the videos or several of them, she saw where Liz first initiated and then made love to Mathew.

Matt never made the first move other than kissing her. Sam sat back to ponder the situation. She was glad that she had talked to Cyndi about birth control. Sex was like the forbidden elixir that once that bottle was opened it was so addictive that you can't put the genie back into the bottle.

She remembered talking to Liz about the difference between the rapes she experienced and having sex with the man, you love. She liked the sex she was having with Matt, but she needed to realize that even though the Plantation was five thousand acres, mostly wooded, there were also cameras everywhere.

Sam looked at Gary and demanded, "Security cameras, there were security cameras in that area, weren't there?" Gary nodded and pointed to another folder, she checked it, and several videos were marked Liz. Sam reached over and just hit Gary but said nothing. Gary looked back and begged, "What was that for?" Sam bitterly replied, "For not telling me, you had her on the other cameras as well.

Sam found about three PTZ cameras or Pan, tilt, and Zoom that were in sight of the spots used by them, and each one had excellent shots of the pair in the woods making love. Sam turned to Gary and demanded, "Has my husband seen these?"

Gary shrugged his shoulders and said, "He has access to those folders from his office, so I don't know if he has seen them or not. He hasn't said anything to me." Sam leaned close and said, "If any more videos appear, you tell me immediately, do you understand?"

Gary nodded then asked, "What do I tell Mr. Paterson, he ordered me not to tell anyone." Sam gave him an angry look and said, "That is my daughter, you tell me first or do I talk to Jamie and Susan?" Gary shook his head quickly; both those women intimidated the hell out of him, and he didn't want them mad at him.

They heard a buzz and Gary looked at the monitor and said, "O-shit!"

CHAPTER 32:
Old friends but a new story

Liz sat back in shock as she looked at Jimmy Dittle sitting in the wheelchair, he was wearing a tattered coat and a blanket covering his lap, and he had gloves with the fingers cut out. Jimmy sat in the chair for several seconds before speaking then said, "Well-well Ms. Raven, how have you been?"

Liz sat and looked at him for a second as her fear screamed at her, then she took hold of her fear, and finally responded, "Doing great, never better until I saw your sorry face." Jimmy looked at her intently then slowly chuckled and asked, "And your mother, how is she doing?" Liz answered with a smirk saying, "She is doing great shooting your dick off did her a world of good."

Seeing Jimmy Dittle for the first time had scared her at first, then Trevor's words came back. There will be a time when the last line of defense will be you. She then remembered her new watch and a sudden thought came to her, there was a trafficking device in that watch.

Jimmy was silent as he studied her, but then, he chuckled and nodded then retorted, "I'm sure there are several women who wanted to do that, but Liz I'm a changed man, I have repented, what can I do to make you forgive me?" Liz's face went blank as she stared at Jimmy then replied, "Die."

This was frustrating Jimmy, so he glanced behind her then back at Liz and said, "Look I'm sorry for what we did, but it was business, just business." Liz continued to study Jimmy and she wasn't buying a word he said then replied, "Just business huh, I tell you what, let me borrow the officer's gun for a minute, but don't worry this will just be business." Jimmy chuckled then looked down then back up and replied, "Touché."

Liz knew she needed to stall. There was a reason Jimmy brought her here, he wanted something otherwise she would have been dead. She knew her father was coming and all she needed to do was to stall as long as possible. Liz looked at Jimmy and asked, "As sickening as it is to see you after all this time, why did you bring me here?"

Jimmy chuckled and replied, "What! I can't say hi to my favorite who… girl?" Liz gave him an angry look and retorted, "You had it right the first time. You made me your whore, and not very nicely either." Jimmy smiled and retorted, "And a fine whore you were."

Liz didn't like being referred to as a whore even though that was what he had made her, but she needed to get to the bottom of this and asked, "As sickening as this conversation is making me, why did you bring me here?" Jimmy sat up straight and looked intently at Liz and finally replied, "Well you see because your lovely mother took it upon herself to destroy my pelvis, I now need multiple operations just so I can walk much less anything else, and they cost money, the money I used to have but don't anymore because someone drained my bank account. I have the feeling the person who did that was you."

Liz didn't want to give anything away with her expression but then said, "Who me, what would give you that idea?" Jimmy looked at her intently then demanded, "Don't lie to me, you took my money!" Liz gave him a quizzical look and then answered, "Now Jimmy think about it, for me to steal your money I would need to open a bank account which I haven't. I would then need to log onto your computer that was taken by the police, to get the passwords. Then into your bank and transfer the money, Jimmy thinks about it, how could I do that?"

Suddenly there was a voice from behind her and soon the person appeared when Captain Fletcher walked up beside her and addressed Jimmy. He glanced down at Liz and then said, "Look Trevor Paterson opened the account and had her transfer the money into it. She knows where the money is and knows how to get it back." Liz looked up at him, she recognized him from the picture her father showed her when they returned from Paris. She studied him for a second then asked, "You're Capt. Fletcher, aren't you?"

The captain looked at her with surprise, then back at Jimmy when Liz continued, "Oh! That money? Please forgive me. You're right Jimmy! I did take your money and put it into the bank account for the Abused Women's Charity. Now I know how that makes you feel but you need to understand Jimmy, it was just business. But I have good news for you, guess who oversees the charity, Jimmy, this guy, he could have written you a check for the money but instead, he had you kidnap me, so Jimmy how does it feel to be fucked like a cheap whore?"

Capt. Fletcher looked at Liz and retorted, "That doesn't matter, I can't just write a check, you have to do it." Liz nodded and replied, "Oh really, now how am I supposed to do that?" Jimmy motioned with his hand and the lead detective walked into the light pushing a roll-around table with a laptop sitting on it. Liz looked up and asked, "Oh the detective that got his ass kicked on my front porch. How's your ego bozo?" The Detective gave her a hard look then walked over to the Captain and Liz heard him whisper, "He's in position."

Liz looked at the laptop sitting on the table then back at Jimmy and said, "Okay here I go, I'm hacking into the bank and I'm going to transfer the money." She then sat back with her hands still handcuffed behind her, and still tied to the chair, she then looked at Jimmy. Jimmy looked at Liz, then at the captain then back at Liz, and then demanded, "She can't type with her hands behind her back, fool!"

The captain looked down at Liz then over at the detective and nodded his head. The detective immediately removed the handcuffs and removed the rope around her chest so she could type. Liz opened the laptop and fired it up then as it was coming up, she asked, "I take it you have Wi-Fi here?" The captain nodded and walked over to Jimmy and whispered to Jimmy.

As soon as the computer came up, Liz was thinking of the commands Gary had been teaching her. The strings of commands performed functions like turning on cameras and microphones, once the laptop was up, she opened a notepad window and started to key in assembler language saved it as a BAT file then clicked on it. There was a flash and the file disappeared. Liz sat and watched the screen and she saw the light for the camera come on. She quickly glanced up then moved the black tape that was covering the camera lens and covered the camera in light.

The captain looked over at Liz and asked, "What are you doing?" Liz was watching the bottom right of the screen for an icon, it suddenly appeared, and she looked up at the captain and asked, "Before I do this, I need some assurances." Jimmy looked up at the captain then back at Liz and demanded, "Like what assurances?" Liz crossed her arms, looked over at the pair, and replied, "So what happens once I transfer the money."

Liz had gained confidence; she knew they needed her to perform the transfer and she needed to stall as long as possible. This realization also allowed her time to lambast them for their ignorance. Also, it gave her time to figure out what the real plan was here. She now knew that the Capt. Could have given Jimmy the money but didn't, why?

Jimmy spoke up saying, "We will let you go of course." Liz looked at him and retorted, "Oh really, and why doesn't that make me feel warm and fuzzy?" Jimmy glanced up at the captain and shot back, "Look you have my word!" Liz gave him a smirk and replied, "Is that the same word you gave my mother if she came to your office to get me?"

Jimmy leaned back in his wheelchair as if he was just hit and looked intently at Liz. Then slowly answered; "If you don't do this; we will rape you into submission like we did the last time." Liz nodded then looked at the captain then over at the detective then asked, "I only see two here who have dicks, so unless you have someone else?"

Jimmy turned to his left and looked into the darkness then slowly the large man from Jimmy's office stepped into the light and stood. Liz nodded and said, "Hi doofus have you recovered from that beat down my friend gave you?" He gave her an ugly look and then stepped back into the darkness.

Liz looked back at Jimmy and said, "As I see it, Jimmy, what you have here is an old fart, who is only good for thirty seconds, Bozo there who prefers children because he isn't equipped to satisfy a woman, and your muscle man, who has been taking steroids for so long he makes a Chihuahua look like a porn star. So, your threat to rape me into submission is just wishful thinking, isn't it?"

Jimmy exploded yelling, "I need my money, you have it, and I want it, check the computer she was typing something earlier!" The captain walked quickly over and turned the table around, so it was facing the other way, Jimmy then looked at the screen but only the normal icons were present. They didn't notice the icon in the bottom right corner showing an external connection.

Gary was looking up into Sam's determined face and was about to say something when they heard a beep and suddenly, they could see Liz sitting in a chair talking to someone behind the computer. She was negotiating with someone then suddenly the computer moved, and they could see Captain Fletcher and Jimmy Dittle.

Sam and Gary looked at each other and Gary called out, "I love her, I could have her children!" Sam gave Gary an incredulous look and asked, "Isn't that medically impossible?" Gary looked at her for a second and nodded yes then said, "Yeah maybe, I don't know but look what she has done, she created a connection to our servers from their computer, damn she is awesome!"

Gary picked up his cell and called Trevor. As they listened to Liz, they heard her address, the captain then Jimmy then she referred to the detectives and the big bodyguard from Jimmy's office and Gary relayed the information.

Liz glanced at the men standing around her then narrowed onto the Detective and asked, "So your friend is in position, I heard you say that earlier, which means he is probably in position outside waiting for my father to arrive so he could take them out."

Liz suddenly realized that this was a trap. The captain needed to take Trevor out so he could do whatever he wanted with the Abused Women Shelter. Liz surmised that once Trevor was taken out, they would then kill Jimmy and his friend then claim they busted a major sex scheme.

Liz then looked at Jimmy and said, "Jimmy, you're a stupid little prick. Sorry, that was insensitive since you don't have one. But you've been played like a cheap trick, you see he knows, I can't get your money back and he has no intention of giving it back. He is using you as bait to get my father here, so he can kill him. That way he will take over the Charity, and you will be blamed for killing my father. Then he will kill you and your friend because you killed me."

Jimmy looked at Liz in shock as the pieces came together in his head, he slowly looked up at the captain and said, "She has a point, she is right, you could have just given me the money, but you came up with this plan, you're playing me." Gary still had Trevor on the phone and relayed the information.

CHAPTER 33:
Establishing order

Trevor was listening intently on the phone and then said, "According to the GPS there are two warehouses at that location, can you get me the blueprints for them?" Trevor listened for a second then clicked off. Trevor looked at the other people in the SUV and started to relay what he had just learned. His tablet beeped and Trevor ordered Susan to pull to the side of the road.

Trevor opened the file that Gary had sent, and Trevor then said, "Liz is here but she said they have someone outside in a sniper position waiting for us." Susan and Jamie looked at each other when Jamie said, "Jeff and I will take out the sniper, the most likely position is here on the roof of the warehouse across the street." Trevor nodded and said, "Then Susan and I will go down the back side of this Warehouse and go in, keep your com gear on, let me know when you have the sniper."

They pulled out and just a few minutes later they turned down a side street then pulled to the side of the road. All four exited the vehicle and geared up. The road dead-ended into a left turn and went in between the two warehouses. Jamie decided to leave her rifle in the vehicle as they checked their pistols and knives.

The four approached and came to the rear of the first warehouse where Liz was, Jamie and Jeff crept to the corner of the building and peeked around then ran across the street to the other warehouse and quietly walked down about one-third its length until they found a metal ladder to the roof.

Jamie led Jeff up the ladder to the roof. Jamie peaked over the edge and saw an air-conditioning structure on the other side of the roof and felt that was the best place for a sniper hide. Jamie gave Jeff a hand motion and then eased over the parapet. Jeff came over the parapet but held his position as Jamie crept toward the hide.

As Jamie rounded the corner of the AC unit, she could see someone lying on the roof with a sniper rifle. Jamie retreated then whispered she had found the sniper. Jeff started forward and Jamie went back around, and dropped onto the sniper with her knee in his back pressed her pistol to his head, and whispered, "Move and you're dead." He froze.

Trevor and Susan went down to the back of the warehouse and found the rear door. Susan pulled her lock-picking kit out and made short work of the lock and they were in. The warehouse was well over a hundred meters long and two stories tall with a row of windows four feet tall just under the roofline.

The second floor was nothing more than a large fifty by thirty-foot room reached by two sets of stairs on each side of the structure that was about one-third down. The walls of the room were half wall then half window and were on all four walls of the second floor but when they looked out the windows, the entire first floor was visible.

Trevor saw the squad car and walked carefully toward it. He motioned for Susan to go up the far stairs as he slowly went up the stairs near the squad car. Trevor heard Jamie say she found the sniper, then heard her say she had him. Trevor was halfway up the stairs and whispered, "Secure him and Jamie, man his rifle and stay there, when I point at someone and say bang, take him out." She said, "Got it" back.

Trevor pulled his pistol from inside his jacket and held it ready as he ascended the stairs, as he neared the door, he peaked through the window to get a lay of the land then backed down hid the weapon in his coat, and whispered, "Is everyone ready." He got three acknowledgments back then he crept back up the stairs and opened the door slowly then slid in.

Trevor heard Liz arguing with Captain Fletcher saying, "So that is the whole point, for you to take over the Charity." Jimmy looked up at the captain saying, "So you never intended to help me, after what I did for you?" The captain walked over to the Detective and ordered, "Call him, see if he has seen anything yet?" The detective picked up a radio and called his friend, he didn't get an answer, so he called again, but still no answer. He looked out the window toward the roofline of the other building.

Trevor was watching him from the dark and heard Jamie in his earwig, "You want me to answer it?" Trevor shook his head no. He knew she was watching him. Trevor looked over and saw a series of lights in a path, so he stepped under the first one and announced, "What's wrong your friend isn't answering?" The detective spun around and when he saw Trevor he pulled his gun and yelled," Freeze!"

Trevor held his hands up and said, "Hold on bud, I'm not armed, you can search me if you like?" The detective glanced at the captain who had pulled his pistol too and the captain motioned with his head for the detective to approach Trevor. Trevor slowly lowered his hand to grab the bottom corners of his jacket and held it open for the detective to search for him.

The black lining made it difficult to see, and with the way Trevor held the jacket, he couldn't see the weapon. The detective gingerly approached and kept as far back as possible as he patted him down. The detective glanced over his shoulder at the captain but when he turned back, he swung at Trevor.

Trevor saw the look in his eye and knew he was going to try this, and as he swung Trevor pushed the punch passed him, spun him around, took the gun away, and then pushed him to the floor. Trevor then turned and walked toward the captain who still had his gun out and just as he got close, Trevor tossed him the pistol and said, "Tell your friend he needs to grow up."

The detective hit the floor and was stunned but when he got back up, he walked quickly toward Trevor. Trevor had tossed the gun he took to the captain and walked on passed. The captain held his hand up and gave the gun back to the detective.

Trevor walked over and stood between Liz and Jimmy Dittle. He looked down at his daughter, and asked, "You, okay?" Liz nodded yes, she was worried about her father, but it looked like he had everything under control. Trevor looked over at Jimmy and said, "I don't think I have had the pleasure?" Liz spoke up and said, "This is Jimmy Dittle, a local dickless scumbag and owner of three fine whorehouses, now closed."

Trevor's expression changed as he looked hard at Jimmy and said, "Dickless, you're the one Samantha shot in the pelvis? You and I are going to talk." Trevor then saw the big man glanced at Jimmy and said, "Is this one of your goons, Jimmy?" Liz interjected saying, "That is the Bozo that Susan beat up." Trevor looked down at Jimmy.

Jimmy just nodded then Trevor looked back at the big man and said, "You know your friend is around here somewhere and I think she is looking forward to seeing you." The man looked grim and replied, "Well I'm likewise." Trevor chuckled and shook his head.

Trevor looked back at the captain and said, "Captain you just fucked up." The detective walked up, shoved his gun into Trevor's face, and said, "You listen to me prick I've had enough of your crap." Trevor smiled and asked, "So I see you use that gun as compensation."

The detective glanced at the captain then back at Trevor and said, "Well I have the gun and you don't." Trevor smiled and replied, "Yes you do, but what you don't have is this." Trevor held up his pointing finger. The detective gave him a funny look and glanced at the captain. He then retorted, "So what, you have a finger, I still have this gun?" Trevor heard Jamie say she had him.

Trevor smiled and looked intently at the detective and said, "But with this finger, all I need to do is point it at someone and say bang." Suddenly there was a tinkle then a thud as the bullet passed through the window then the detective's head, the detective's face looked shocked then dropped dead on the floor. Trevor looked away from the captain and whispered, "Get over here now."

The captain was shocked at what happened and started to bring his pistol up at Trevor but Trevor's hand shot out and grabbed the barrel of the pistol and shoved it away before he could pull the trigger then holding the barrel tight he brought it back keeping the gun pointing away and leveraged it out of the Captain's grip then continued to turn it until he pinned the trigger finger within the trigger guard then twisted more until he broke the finger. The captain gave out a yell as everyone heard the snap.

Trevor then jerked the gun out of the captain's hand, Trevor then flipped the pistol and pointed toward the big man on the other side who was approaching fast and said, "Were you going, big fella?" The big man stopped and stood looking at Trevor. Trevor then punched the captain, who fell to the floor.

Jimmy Dittle then spoke up and said, "Okay, since we can't get my money then there is no reason for us to be here. Bruno, help me get out of here." Trevor held his hand up to the big man, and stepped over to look at Jimmy, and said, "Not until we have our talk."

Jimmy looked up at Trevor and fear came over him. He knew who Trevor was. He saw on the News that he had married Samantha Raven. Jimmy had planned then kidnapped and raped his daughter then made her a whore before kidnapping his wife. He knew he wouldn't be on Trevor's Christmas card list.

Jimmy: looked up at Trevor and pleaded, "What are you going to do to me?" Trevor looked at Jimmy and said, "We will talk now." Then he looked at the big man and said, "Like I said earlier there is someone here that is looking forward to seeing you." The big man looked around the dark room then said, "I'm ready." Trevor smiled and said, "Good then stay right there, and she will be along shortly." Trevor heard Susan ask, "You want me to come in?" Trevor was looking at Jimmy when he nodded yes.

Trevor looked at Jimmy and asked, "Jimmy let's tally up the list, you kidnapped my daughter, beat her, raped her, then sold her, then you made a promise to my wife, and reneged on it, then tried to rape her. So, tell me Jimmy what should I do with you?"

The door opened when Jamie and Jeff with the other detective came in. Jamie forced the other detective to kneel so that he and the captain were now kneeling side by side. The two police officers glanced at each other and then hung their heads.

Trevor glanced over at Jamie and said, "Great the whole family is here." Trevor then turned back to the big guy then looked at Jimmy and asked, "Bozo, no that's not what you called him." Trevor pretended to think then looked at him again and said, "Bruno, that's it, your Bruno, right?" Bruno gave him a condescending look and nodded yes. Trevor smiled and said, "So are you ready to get your ass kicked?" Bruno looked left then right and said, "I don't see her."

Suddenly all the lights came on in the room. The big man looked around then turned to look behind him and there beside the door was Susan her hand still on the long series of light switches.

He looked back at Trevor then back at Susan and said, "I don't have any weapons." Susan gave him a small smile then released the buckle of her utility belt and allowed it to fall to the floor. Susan took a step forward and then said, "Now, neither do I."

CHAPTER 34:
Susan proves her metal

Bruno looked over his shoulder at Trevor when Susan announced, "He is mine, I will deal with him." Trevor nodded then stepped to Jimmy. Trevor looked down at Jimmy and asked, "What is the worst way you can think of, to die?" Jimmy smirked and replied, "What does it matter if I end up dead anyway." Trevor smiled and said, "Just the amount of time you get to think about what you have done to deserve to die?"

Susan eyed the big man as she stepped to her left, it had been around six months since their last run-in, and she was curious if he had completely healed. What she noticed was that he had worked hard to get ready, he had several advantages over her, being larger, heavier, stronger, and meaner, she had to nullify those by being quicker and smarter. Physically fighting didn't go to the biggest and strongest, it went to the smartest.

As she moved Bruno suddenly leaped forward to push her back, he was trying to get her on the floor and under him which would give him an immediate advantage but instead of hitting the floor, she fell back into one of the many posts used to hold up the ceiling in the large room.

He slammed Susan into the post, the post bent, and the ceiling rattled but stayed up. He then tried to use his power punches to beat her down. He held her in place with his shoulder then tried to deliver several hard punches into her abdomen hoping to break her resolve quickly.

Susan was shifting her body to absorb the punches then delivered an elbow to the back of his head and then a knee into his face. Bruno countered by coming up and delivered a hard right into her face knocking her sideways then continued to fire off blows to her face, chest, and gut. Susan couldn't stop the blows but took them and allowed them to push her back.

Jamie looked at Jeff and pointed two fingers at her eyes then at the two Athens policemen, and then as she moved past Liz, she cut the tape tying her to the chair. She then continued over to keep a watch on the fight. Trevor backed up to Liz and asked, "You want to do it or let me?" Liz took the captain's pistol and moved closer then said, "Me, now tell me Jimmy when I was on the floor crying from the beating you gave me, did you feel any remorse?" Jimmy looked at Liz and responded, "Never sweat heart, you're just a piece of meat I can sell, hell you bitches are better than drugs, easy to transport, make more profit, and easy to dispose of."

His words slapped her face as he had done that evening in his office. He didn't care then; he didn't care now. Liz looked back at her father and asked, "Where is the best place to shoot him so he dies slowly?" Trevor was standing behind her, he wanted to see how bloodthirsty she was, sometimes revenge helps in the healing process, but the best healing comes from forgiveness. Jimmy was now trying to anger Liz to get her to end him quickly. No one wants to die slowly.

Trevor stepped up beside her and after glancing at Susan then said, "I like putting one bullet through his rib cage here and one here. That way his lungs will begin to collapse with each breath, and as they collapse, they apply pressure on his heart and diaphragm making it harder to breathe, if you put a hole in the outside of each chest, he will suffocate in five or ten minutes."

Bruno was winning, he had just connected again to Susan's head knocking her onto her back, he jumped in an attempt to land on top of her, but she quickly rolled to one side. She then jumped back onto him as he tried to use his strength to push her off, but she delivered an elbow to his head and then rolled over trying to get his arm into an Arm Bar and break it.

Bruno realized what she was doing and rolled away to stand knowing now that he was no match for her on the floor. He had to take her to standing up. She couldn't withstand his punches for long and that would be his key to victory. Susan already had blood on her cheeks and one eye swelling, she had taken a beating so far. Bruno could see his punches were having the desired effect, but it wasn't over.

Susan jumped up as well and then saw him barreling toward her again. His punches were causing damage. She or any woman couldn't withstand many of those punches, so she needed to change her tactics. As he barreled forward, she waited until he was right upon her, when she dropped down taking him over her hip and flipping him onto his back. He landed hard and was stunned when Susan jumped forward and delivered two hard punches to his eyes. She had to blind him if she could.

Liz turned to Trevor and handed him the pistol and said, "I'm sorry but I want him dead but I'm not able to do it. Trevor pulled her into a hug and said, "That is fine honey, taking another's life is not easy and should be considered carefully, if you're not ready then I'm not going to force you."

Trevor stood and looked down at Jimmy and said, "But I don't have that problem." He looked over at Susan and Bruno still fighting and didn't want to do anything to interrupt them. He knelt before Jimmy and said, "Jimmy, many years ago some people murdered my parents, and what I did to them stopped a lot of killing in the area, they didn't know who I was, but they didn't want to end up like the men I killed." He gave Jimmy a wicked grin that sent shivers down Jimmy's back.

Susan jumped away when Bruno jumped back up, and he turned quickly and swung a power punch that would floor any man. Susan saw him advertise the punch and quickly ducked under the swing then stepped in and delivered a hard punch to his eye then another to his rib cage where she had either cracked or broken them the last time. The air went out of Bruno when she connected to his rib cage, and she learned that the ribs hadn't completely healed from their last fight.

Bruno delivered a quick jab and tried another power punch, but Susan was now getting her game on and had him measured, she knew exactly how close she could come to dodge his punches while delivering hers. Susan was now working him left and right, she would move him one way only to jump back the other way when he attacked, and then deliver a kick into that rib again or a punch into his eye.

Bruno was now dropping his left arm trying to protect that rib but that left his left eye open to attack. Susan would jump right when he threw a right punch, she would jump left and deliver a jab to his left eye. Then when he raised his right arm to throw a right haymaker she would duck under the arm and deliver a punch into the middle of his upper arm hitting the nerve. If she could hit it, several times the nerve would stop all feeling in that arm and take his power away.

Susan was now bouncing around, when he threw a punch, she would use her speed to counter the punch and hit him somewhere that hurt. He tried a wide swing with his left and Susan spun and delivered a back kick to that rip again. He was now wheezing from her last kick to his side.

Susan was now circling him and picking him apart. He had overplayed his hand, and he knew he was in deep trouble. Susan was dodging and weaving, and he couldn't keep up. He was now backing up when Susan stepped to one side and she punched him with her right hand, not wanting to move his left arm from his left side, which left him open down the center. Susan let the punch come then spun low sending a Mike Tyson uppercut and forcing him back again.

Bruno was now fighting with only one arm, and every time he punched out with it, Susan would punch into that nerve on the inside of his upper arm, it was throbbing with pain, and he had no strength in it. He was trying to block her punches with his hands, but his eyes were also closing, and by the time he saw the punch it was landing, his head was bouncing off the post behind him. The only reason he was still standing was that he had locked his knees and thrown all his weight into the post.

Susan then stepped in and delivered several punches of left and right, then an uppercut that would make Mike Tyson proud. With his legs locked, he was doing everything he could to keep himself vertical until Susan jumped up and came down with a boot into his left knee snapping it and the leg gave out throwing him onto the floor, the pain was too much, and he lost consciences. Susan backed away and took a deep breath. She hadn't had a fight that hard since that bitch Rhonda Rousey beat her. Jamie jumped up and squealed, then threw her arms around Susan and congratulated her.

Susan had to hold up one hand saying, "Careful girlfriend, I'm hurting pretty bad." They looked at each other and laughed. Jamie looked at Bruno lying on the floor and said, "Yeah but you beat him girl, you beat him like a dirty rug."

The captain took the opportunity to try to jump up, but Jeff had stepped back, and when the captain jumped up Jeff delivered a strike with the butt of the rifle knocking him to the floor. Trevor turned quickly and pointed the captain's pistol at him. Trevor nodded and asked, "Susan can you move?" Susan was wiping the blood from her face and replied, "No problem, let's get out of here."

Trevor stood about ten feet away from Jimmy and said, "Jimmy I wish I could say it was a pleasure, but it wasn't." Trevor raised the pistol and shot Jimmy in the outside of his chest on the left then followed by one on the right. Jimmy looked shocked and in pain as he tried to cover the wounds to no avail. Trevor then grabbed the captain by his collar, pulled him up, and forced him toward Jimmy in the wheelchair. Captain Fletcher looked at Jimmy and then said, "Couldn't happen to a nicer fellow."

He looked up at Trevor who had traded weapons with Jeff and was holding the rifle at his waist he pointed it at the captain who looked surprised and asked, "What are you doing?" Trevor said, "Remember when I said that if you double-crossed me, the consequences would be dire?" The captain held up both hands with his palms up and said, "But I brought you Jimmy D. . . ."

Trevor smiled and replied, "Not good enough." Trevor pulled the trigger hitting the captain in the center of his chest. As he went down Trevor handed the rifle back to Jeff and took the captain's pistol saying, "Wipe that down." He then looked at the other detective on his knees he said, "Stand up." The detective started to cry and pleaded, "But I didn't . . ." he never finished as Trevor shot him in the chest. He walked over to Jamie and held out the pistol saying, "You want to do the honors?" Jamie didn't flinch, she took the pistol, stepped over to Bruno on the floor, and shot him in the head.

Trevor looked at Jeff and said, "Place the rifle into his hands." Trevor was pointing at the sniper then stepped over to the captain and using his handkerchief, he wiped his prints off the weapon and placed the weapon into his hands. As Trevor finished with the captain, he instructed Liz to grab the laptop as Jeff wiped the chair down. Trevor picked up the first detective's pistol and wiped his prints off then placed it back into his hands.

Trevor looked around making a mental note to ensure all evidence of them was not left then motioned for everyone to leave. Trevor used his handkerchief to turn off the lights as they left.

No one said a word as they walked out of the building through the back door. Trevor picked up Liz and carried her since she had lost her shoes earlier. When they reached the SUV, they climbed in and headed home.

CHAPTER 35:
Making sure it is ended

They made their way down the stairs and then to the back door. Once everyone was through the door, Jeff locked it and headed toward the SUV. Jamie helped Susan into the passenger seat as Trevor, Jeff, and Liz climbed into the back seat. They headed back to the plantation, and no one spoke until Liz looked up at her father who was staring at nothing outside the window.

Liz reached over and wrapped her arms around Trevor's arm and snuggled into him then said, "I'm sorry I couldn't shoot Jimmy." Trevor turned and looked down at her smiled and replied, "That's Okay, killing someone is not easy, it is not something I take lightly."

Liz could see the far-off look in his eyes and asked, "You made it look easy." Trevor glanced up at Jeff, the large black man, who was a retired SEAL and had gone into situations where death occurred, regularly. Jeff glanced over at Trevor who was sitting on the other side of Liz and because of the close quarters and quiet, it was hard not to hear everything. Trevor nodded and replied, "When I saw who was in there, I decided to kill them. I knew if I didn't end it tonight, they would be back. Besides they made the mistake of attacking my family."

Liz looked at her father and asked, "I don't understand, I never did anything to him, why did they want to hurt us?" Trevor glanced over at Jeff again and saw the small smile on his face. Jeff knew the answer, but it was Trevor's turn to answer it. Trevor looked down at his daughter and replied, "Some people are just evil, and the only way to deal with them is harshly. If you try to be nice, they will take it as a weakness and come back again. You saw that with Jimmy Dittle and the captain. They had already experienced the power that I, and my people can bring, but they came back to test it again. Sometimes the best way to deal with people like that is to just eliminate them. If I allowed any of them to live, we would be seeing them again."

Liz looked up at her father then she snuggled in closer to Trevor. He raised his arm, pulled her close to his side, and held her. Liz looked up and asked, "What about Matt?" Trevor looked over at Jeff. Jeff pulled his phone, called the Mansion, and asked, "What is Matt's status?" He listened for a few seconds then said, "Okay." He looked at Liz and said, "They brought Matt to the mansion, he's got some cracked ribs and a concussion, but he will be Okay. Mrs. Paterson called his parents and asked if he could spend the night. He refuses to go to sleep or home until you arrive." Liz smiled.

In a short time, they pulled in front of the Mansion and Jamie helped Susan out of the vehicle and into the Mansion. Jeff grabbed the gear out of the back and followed them in. Trevor grabbed a duffle bag in one hand, wrapped his arm around Liz, and then went into the mansion.

Gary met them in the foyer and asked, "I guess it all went well?" Trevor released Liz when she saw Matt with bandages on, so she ran to him. Trevor filled Gary in on the situation when Samantha walked over and told Liz, "Okay honey, we need to let Matt go to his room to get some rest, and you need to go take a bath as well." Liz nodded and kissed Matt on his cheek then walked off with Samantha.

Trevor smiled at Sam and Liz gave Matt a wave as they disappeared into the elevator. Trevor turned back to Gary and asked, "She questioned you about those videos, didn't she?" Gary glanced up at Matt who had moved closer then nodded his head, and replied, "Yeah, she did Boss, and I tried to put her off but you know how she is." Matt was listening, and didn't understand and asked, "What videos?"

Trevor ignored Matt but chuckled and asked, "So what did you tell her?" Gary looked nervous and replied, "I let her look at them, and she said she will take it up with you later." Trevor chuckled and retorted, "Yeah you caved like a cardboard box." Matt was looking at both men and still didn't understand. Gary looked up at Trevor and pleaded, "Ah come on boss, you know how I am around women, besides she threatened to turn Jamie loose on my ass, and that woman scares the hell out of me."

Trevor chuckled again then patted Gary on his back as Matt asked again, "What videos?" Gary looked up at Matt with a glance at Trevor and replied, "There are two cameras in the cab of the truck and four more on the outside."

Matt's face went white and with a slight stutter queried, "M …my truck." Trevor interjected saying, "Look the cameras are only there for security reasons and since you and Liz never did anything, so you have nothing to worry about, right?"

Matt glanced at Gary who was giving him a side glance and nodded, "No sir, they only talked and laughed, I never saw them do anything... no sir." Then he gave Matt another side glance. Matt nodded and repeated, "No sir, you know how much I respect and admire your daughter, I would never do anything, no sir."

Trevor looked at Gary and asked, "Which room you got him in?" Gary looked up at Trevor and replied, "205, I was going to take him up." Trevor pulled the room key from Gary's hand and said, "Na don't bother, you have been up late and need to rest, you take off and I will show him the room." Gary glanced at Matt and nodded then replied, "Okay sir, it is no problem as you like."

As Gary walked up one set of stairs, Matt and Trevor went up the other set of stairs to the second floor then the first room off the foyer was 205. Trevor unlocked the door checked to make sure it was clean and ready then turned to Matt and patted him on the back while saying, "Okay you crash here, there's stuff in the refrigerator if you need it and I will see you in the morning." Matt nodded and said, "Thank you, sir."

His heart was in his throat when he learned that there were cameras in the truck, which meant they had to have seen him get to first, then second, and third base with Liz. Then he remembered the day after the big game against Gainesville when Liz accompanied him to patrol the fence and ended up making love in a small clearing directly behind the truck. Matt thought to himself "Oh shit!"

When Trevor entered his bedroom, he found Samantha lying in bed naked like a plump egg. He smiled and thought that most men wouldn't think that was sexy, but he knew she was carrying his child, and that made her sexy. He also knew he was going to get the third degree and she was pulling out all stops to make sure he told her everything. Trevor smiled at her then went into the bathroom and climbed into the shower. He had just lathered up when the door opened, and Samantha climbed in.

Trevor smiled at her and said, "Couldn't wait for me huh." Sam gave a seductive smile and retorted, "Why wait when I can get you started right here." Sam did interrogate Trevor and didn't stop until he told her all about the cameras and the videos.

Matt lay down on the queen bed and was staring at the ceiling when he heard a light knock on the door. The apartments had three rooms with a living room/kitchen area then a bedroom and bathroom off it. Matt padded in his bare feet and undershorts to the front door, he opened it slightly only to see Liz, who at once pushed it open, and she squeezed in.

Matt looked at her with fear in his eyes and said, "Liz you can't be in here, if your dad catches you in here, he will kill me." Liz smiled then pushed the door closed and locked it, she guided him over to a chair at the table and pushed him into it then sat in his lap facing him and said, "Don't worry, they are both in the shower, they don't know I'm down here."

Matt looked at the door then at Liz and asked, "How did you find me?" Liz giggled and said, "I came down and was knocking on the doors, then Jamie stepped out of the shadows and almost scared the life out of me, she said I would save a lot of time by coming to this door."

Matt with fear in his eyes looked again at the door then at Liz and asked, "So Jamie knows you're in here, Oh God I'm a dead man." Matt then looked at Liz and said, "I heard your dad talking about videos, there were cameras in the truck, they could have seen us?"

Liz smiled and nodded then said, "Yeah mom told me." Matt's eyes flew open even more and asked, "She did what? Oh my God your mother knows!" Liz smiled and said, "Oh yeah what we didn't realize is all those camera pods we see out there, well those cameras move and tilt and zoom in real close."

The only thing that kept Matt in the chair was Liz sitting in his lap as he painfully asked, "How close?" Liz replied, "They can read the name on your underwear as I pulled them off." All Matt could say was, "Oh God I'm dead!" as his head fell into Liz's chest. Liz chuckled and held him and petted the back of his head then said, "Yeah Mom was pretty upset, she told Gary that she was to be notified of any more videos, or she would sic Jamie and Susan on his ass."

Matt with his head still on her chest asked, "How many videos do they have of us." Liz was still straddling him and slid closer then answered, "Well that first time behind your truck?" Matt nodded and said, "Yeah they got us by the camera in the rear of the truck." Liz nodded then said, "Well we had three of those pods on us, and from what my mother says, it was good enough for armature porn." Matt looked up at Liz and asked, "Honey I'm so sorry, I never realized those cameras would have been able to see us." Liz smiled and replied, "Well Mom said that Gary said that no one has seen them, so you're safe for now."

Matt could smell her perfume and feel her body holding him close, which was the only reason he wasn't crying, if he was going to die, he might as well enjoy his last few moments alive. He looked up into Liz's face and said, "Your father is going to kill me and bury me in the woods."

Liz stood up and said, "Come on, it's not that bad, we just have to be more careful in the future." Matt didn't know what to say, he was a dead man walking, Liz guided him to the bed pushed him onto it then reached up and pulled his underwear off and as she climbed in with him, he asked, "Is this my last rights you're giving me?" Liz smiled as she pulled her nightgown off showing she was now naked as well and said, "There are no cameras in here."

Matt pulled her close to him as he hovered over her and asked, "This is the worst secret, if I'm going to die, then I might as well make this my last meal." Liz giggled and said, "Oh! I don't think Daddy will kill you, he might torture you for a while." Matt gave her a sullen look and retorted, "Terrific sentiment coming for the girl he loves, I'm just the guy defiling his daughter, it isn't the same." Liz giggled again.

Susan and Jamie were standing in the hallway and Susan asked, "Why did you tell her where he was?" Jamie smiled and replied, "What if she knocked on Gary's door, and he opened it naked." Susan chuckled and said, "Yeah after feasting on Matt so many times, a view like that could blind her." Jamie chuckled and retorted, "My sentiments exactly."

CHAPTER 36:
Epilogue

Matt persevered and continued working at the Plantation. He and Liz became an inseparable pair in and out of school, even though Trevor still didn't trust the high school to keep her safe. After Liz had ruined the football career of two players, no one dared to mess with her again. Bullies never mess with anyone willing to fight back.

The dynamic duo quickly became proficient in martial arts, driving, and languages. Trevor sent them to stay at the Chalet in Paris and the Olive Plantation in southern Spain to practice their French and Spanish.

The Winder football team made it to the district championship, but without Matt, they lost to Gainesville. However, the next year, they beat Gainesville during the regular season and defeated them by a fourth-quarter field goal during Winder's first championship. Mathew was offered several college scholarships to prestigious schools, including Alabama, Georgia, and Clemson.

In February, Samantha delivered an 8 lb. 2 oz baby boy named Trevor Junior, or TJ for short. Sam also talked to Cynthia Winston, and it turned out that her husband, Dr. Jeb Winston, was a urologist. She made an appointment, and Trevor was supposed to keep it. It was never confirmed if he did or not.

Samantha also delved into Trevor's financials and soon discovered that her previous assumptions were wrong. Paterson Corp. was a U.S. Corporation, and it consisted of some fast-food chains, hotels, two different grocery store chains, and some investments made into Georgia moviemakers. His second company was Paterson Global which had three subsidiaries outside of the U.S. There was Paterson Euro. Paterson Asia and Paterson America.

Paterson Euro consisted of automobile manufacturing in Germany, France, Italy, and Israel. He also had shipbuilding companies in Norway, Italy, and Spain. Furthermore, he owned several hotels and resorts throughout Europe as well as Morgenstern Financial in Israel.

Paterson Asia had resorts In Japan, Vietnam, Thailand, Korea, and Australia. Additionally, Trevor owned several electronics manufacturing companies in those same countries along with a few other construction and shipbuilding operations. It soon became apparent that the U.S. business was valued at well over four billion, while his overseas investments were upwards of ten billion. Liz was stunned when she suddenly realized the extent of his investments.

Paterson America consisted of holdings in Central and South America. He owned construction, shipbuilding, Hotels and Resorts, as well as manufacturing in several different countries. In addition, some power plants in Panama.

Samantha discovered that Trevor had invested in LG and Samsung and assisted both in fostering inroads into the U.S. and world markets. He was also integral to Hyundai becoming a major player. Additionally, Trevor played a hand in Tata Motors of India's purchase of Jaguar and Rover. He helped them, in not only securing the two auto lines but also in preserving their prestige.

Life continued for the family as everyone settled into their schedules. Liz and Matt were still spending four hours per day in the gym. They studied several martial arts skills, such as Wing Chun, Kickboxing, and Judo. Jamie also introduced Kendo, the art of Japanese sword fighting. She had attempted to incorporate it into the training earlier, but since Liz took a liking to it, she decided to intensify the studies with more training. This training included using weapons like brooms, mop handles, and baseball bats as weapons for defense.

No one could predict the path of the future, but it was coming. As the past six months have shown, you can't hide from what is going to happen, but you can be sure that adventure, danger, and mystery are inevitable. The only alternative is to prepare yourself in every way possible.

It will be two years before Elizabeth faces another daunting test of her abilities. But what has happened during this year convinced her that she's capable. With this experience, she now knows that her father was right and that the training and exercise are making her a force. With that, her confidence and courage improved.

She will be challenged by men who are almost twice her size, and she will have to hide her identity to protect herself and her family. Her mother will be there for part of it, but Liz will eventually discover her path. The trajectory of this path will be something unexpected, but it is coming. People and organizations will attempt to break her physically, and mentally, as no woman has been tested before.

Will she prevail as she maneuvers through the gauntlet of trouble headed her way?

Elizabeth Raven; Coming into her own

CHAPTER 1:
Unknown Attackers

It was now two years later in early March, and the cold had settled into the Northern Georgia landscape, bringing a cold snap that required the women to wear long pants and warm coats to brave the outside elements. The day was overcast as the clouds were trying to make up their minds on whether to rain or snow.

Samantha and Elizabeth had chosen this day, Elizabeth's seventeenth birthday, to venture out to Buford and explore the Mall of Georgia in all of its glory. What is more relaxing for two beautiful women than shopping with someone else's money? The pretense was that they needed some dresses, but they actually purchased items for everyone else at the mansion. Their gift to themselves was mother-daughter bonding time.

Samantha and Elizabeth had come to live at the Mansion on the Plantation had been absorbed into life and the eclectic group of people there, but today, they needed a break. They drove to the Mall of Georgia and perused the various shops and stores before stopping for lunch at the food court.

They were swimming in a sea of humanity in its own anonymity and loving it, but not everyone was anonymous. As they sat at Orange Julius giggling, Liz quietly leaned forward and whispered, "That guy leaning against the fountain with a red cap---this is the third time I've seen him." Sam giggled and replied, "Yea, and there is a man in a yellow ball cap about 50 ft behind you that has been turning up as well. Call Gary and let him know."

Gary was in the control room at the Mansion, when Liz speed-dialed him, "Oh Martha, hi! Hey, I want to know if you were bringing your two friends over tonight." Gary recognized the code word and asked, "What is your current location?" Liz smiled and replied, "So Luis Orange is coming? Terrific!"

Gary hacked into the camera network at the mall and started to bring up the cameras around Orange Julius, scanning the crowd.

Gary asked, "Can you give me something to pick them out?" Liz glanced at her mother and said, "No, I don't like the yellow dress, but I can wear the red one?" Gary hit a couple of keys, and suddenly, the cameras within the mall appeared on the 60" LED screen. He quickly narrowed in on the cameras near the Orange Julius.

He spotted men in several colors of caps. "Is one standing by the fountain?" Liz smiled and replied, "Uh-huh." Gary grabbed screenshots of several men and started running them through the face recognition program. On another monitor, he pulled up a map of the mall and pinpointed Sam and Liz's location in the mall.

Sam and Liz continued their banter, and soon Gary came back, asking, "So you parked at the agreed-upon spot?" Liz giggled again and gave a seductive, "Yea!" Gary picked up another phone and speed-dialed a number. He introduced himself and continued to talk on both lines simultaneously, "I need a taxi at the front of the Mall of Georgia right now . . ."

He then addressed Liz. "Liz, wait five minutes. Slowly walk out the front of the mall, and casually head to the parking lot." Then the other voice gave him a number, and Gary forwarded it. "There will be a cab waiting---number 1151. Get in and tell him where to go." Liz giggled and said, "Okay, sweets! See you soon."

She hung up, looked at her watch, and leaned over towards her mother. "Five minutes out front." Sam put her hand up to her mouth to pretend to hide another giggle. After five minutes, they casually picked up their bags while they slowly walked and talked about the stores as they headed to the front of the mall.

The two men glanced at each other and deftly followed them out of the mall. Just as they left the Mall of Georgia, they pretended to be causal as they sauntered towards the parking lot. A cab suddenly appeared. Liz spied the number, 1151, and nodded to it.

The taxi driver popped the trunk lid and then exited the vehicle. Two men approached, but the cab driver knew he was to pick up Liz and Sam and waved them off. Liz spotted him as he opened the rear door and watched her. Liz and Sam threw their shopping bags into the trunk, and Liz slammed it shut.

Sam climbed into the near side while Liz trotted to the opposite side and jumped in. As the cab pulled away, Sam reached over and handed the driver a $50. "We need to go around to Belk's, and hurry!"

The driver turned right and headed to the lane that surrounded the mall. As they approached Belk's, Liz said, "Go to the white Land Cruiser." They exited the cab into the biting cold and retrieved their purchases from the trunk. Liz hit the Fob while Sam climbed into the passenger side and Liz into the driver's side, tossing their packages into the backseat.

Seat belts went on, doors locked, the engine came to life, and they quickly exited the Mall of Georgia parking lot, turning right onto Piedmont. Liz quickly accelerated and turned left to exit onto Woodward Crossing Blvd. before hanging a quick right onto Buford Drive.

They continued down Buford and exited onto I-985, accelerating to 70 mph. They drove several miles before turning onto 129 heading southeast. The Land Cruiser had a turbo charged V8 with front and rear reinforced bumpers. It was not a hardened vehicle, but it was equipped with hydrostatic shocks absorbers and stabilizers. There were buttons on the dash numbered from one to five---one gave a soft ride, and each one intensified until five, which made the suspension almost solid.

The hydrostatic shock absorbers were first developed by DARPA (Defense Advanced Research Project Agency) for the military and the

HumVee. They are filled with a graphite liquid solution that caused them to stiffen when an electrical current is applied.

The bumpers were also specially designed by Trevor Paterson and supported by a steel beam behind the factory bumper. They began to relax, thinking they had lost the two men and laughed at their escape.

When Liz first noticed the SUV, it was approaching at a high rate of speed. She was maintaining the speed limit and expected the vehicle to pass, but it didn't. The SUV was a GMC suburban, and she suspected it was equipped with a large, V8 engine. It was all black with darkened windows on the sides, but the front and rear windows were clear.

It had standard bumpers and equipment. Just before it made contact, Liz yelled out, "Hold on, mom!" Samantha grabbed the "O-shit handle" above the door and pressed back into the seat and headrest when the larger vehicle hit it and propelled the Land Cruiser forward several feet. Liz was holding firmly onto the steering wheel with both hands to ensure that the vehicle remained in a straight line.

The ramming vehicle kept accelerating, making contact again. It started pushing the Land Cruiser forward, and it swayed on the soft suspension. Liz reached over and pressed the two buttons on the suspension then applied her brakes to slow them down without locking the wheels. Samantha yelled out, "What's going on?!"

Liz countered, "I don't know, but this guy rammed us on purpose, so hold on."

Sam glanced at her daughter and looked behind them with fear all over her face. She was scared, but she had faith in Liz. Elizabeth glanced into the rearview mirror and locked eyes with the driver. In an instant, she could see the callous intentions in those eyes. He reminded Liz of the men who had kidnapped her, raped her, and forced her into prostitution.

The fear, humiliation, and anger she had buried in the past came flooding back. No man would ever treat her or any other women like that again, and these men were attempting to do harm to her and her mother. Her nerves steeled, and she knew what she had to do. These men, whoever they were, were going to regret attacking her.

CHAPTER 2:
The Battle Begins

Liz was still a quiet and shy girl. That part never changed, but she had a dark side. Whenever she was presented, with a misogynist, it struck a spot deep in her soul. Like when two football players dragged her into the area behind the theater in order to have their way with her. Because of the training of Jamie and Susan, she put them both into the hospital.

Liz was reluctant at first, but Trevor talked her into trying it. Soon she learned to enjoy the calisthenics and weight training.

Jamie schooled Liz in the art of Wing Chun, and she was sparring with the men on the Plantation in no time. The only problem with sparring against Liz is the fine line she crossed when escalating the fighting intensity. With her speed and strength, she was dangerous. Jamie and Susan had to work with her to channel her rage and learn how to not get angry but get even.

Liz had learned to deliver her punches to specific points--accuracy was important. When she delivered a punch, it hurt, and her accuracy was deadly. The men didn't want to spar with her because she was first, the boss's daughter, and second, she was lethal. Jamie and Susan impressed upon her that she would always be weaker and smaller than her opponent, but she could use her lack of size to trick them into underestimating her abilities.

The two vehicles approached a turn to the left. As they neared the curve, the suburban backed off and accelerated, slamming them again in an attempt to push the vehicle forward into a skid. Liz cursed aloud and hit the gas. The turbocharged V8 in the land cruiser leaped forward into the turn, giving her a small gap between both vehicles.

Liz hit the third button to stiffen the suspension again and eased off the gas. She cut the steering wheel hard into the corner, causing the back to slide out into a sideways skid before hitting the gas again to accelerate out of turn. The attacker wasn't expecting this move, and had to apply brakes to make the curve, which put even more distance between him and the Land Cruiser. The driver of the suburban quickly cut his steering hard into the curve but didn't get the sideways slide he wanted. However, he was able to make it through the curve. His intention was to force the Land Cruiser into a skid and cause them to wreck, but Liz's quick action prevented it.

As he exited the curve, the Land Cruiser had gained expensive distance, which he had to make up. He accelerated towards the vehicle, but, his front bumper was now bent, and one headlight along with the front grill was damaged. Liz, after gaining distance, let off the gas and allowed the Land Cruiser to slow to the speed limit. She kept glancing back at the closing vehicle as they approached again.

Sam looked up and yelled, "Why are you slowing down?" Liz glanced into the rearview mirror "Because, I can't defeat him from the front." Sam, with fear all over her face, replied, "What?! To hell with defeating them---let's get out of here!" Liz was now entering her zone, calculating their approach, and developing a plan.

Sun Tzu, author of "The Art of War," says the best defense is often a better offense.

The attacker was now closing in again and came up behind the land cruiser, only this time; they swerved left into the other lane. Liz looked to her left and saw the young man in the passenger seat. He had lowered his window so they could obtain a clearer view of each other.

He had shaggy black hair that needed to be cut and a three-day beard. As he looked to his right at Liz, he gave her a smirk and blew her a kiss. The Suburban swerved right into the Toyota, hoping she would lose control, but Liz held firmly onto the steering wheel and steered into the attack to absorb the initial impact. Once Liz had countered his attack, she pushed him back. They slammed into her again, trying to force them off the road, but Liz cut to the left and pushed back into them. Both vehicles weighed nearly the same, but the tires of the Land Cruiser were wider, giving it a little more traction. This gave Liz an added advantage, and it was a stalemate as they headed into the straightway.

They continued to try to push the Toyota off the road, but Liz wouldn't let them over. Both drivers saw the logging truck coming, but Liz was on the right side of the road, and the suburban wasn't. The man in the passenger seat looked over at Liz, and she gave him a fiendish smile. They watched as the truck closed the distance at lightning speed. Liz and her adversary were hitting speeds of seventy mph while the logging truck was cruising at 55 mph, making a closing speed of 115 mph.

The logging truck driver blew his horn in a panic until the suburban finally swerved out of desperation into a ditch on the left to avoid being French kissed by a ten-ton truck. Sam looked back at the SUV and then at Liz. "Way to go, girl! Now let's go home."

The Suburban had to spin its wheels but was able to pull back onto the highway and roar back after Liz and Sam. It didn't take long before they pulled alongside and tried to ram them again. Liz immediately tapped her brakes. The SUV shot past them and almost ran off the right side of the road.

This maneuver caused the attacker to pass them, and Liz accelerated after them. Sam yelled, "What are you doing now?!" Liz countered, "Now, I have the advantage." Liz's hard, intent expression slowly softened as a smile crept across her face. She had now arrived in the recessed of her dark space, where she was most lethal. She now had the advantage, so she accelerated up behind them then slammed into the attacker.

Liz hit the Suburban hard and pushed him left then right to see if they would lose control. The attacker wasn't expecting this move and fishtailed. Liz eased up; thinking he would wreck, but he regained control. Liz smiled and whispered to herself, "Okay, so you can drive too." Sam asked, "Is that all you're going to do?"

"I'm just getting started." Liz accelerated again started to pass, but the suburban swerved left to prevent her from passing. Liz smiled and said aloud, "So you think keeping me behind you is an advantage?" Sam glanced over at her daughter and knew where she was. Her mousy daughter was no mouse anymore. She was a lioness about to roar.

Liz slammed into the suburban and pushed them again.

She went left, and the Suburban moved left then jerked right. The Suburban moved right as well. They had to allow another vehicle to pass them by, and Liz tried again. This time, Liz only faked the maneuver and went left again. She began pulling alongside, but instead of passing, she swerved into the back-rear panel between the bumper and the rear wheel, turning harder into the vehicle.

This maneuver forced the vehicle's rear to move right; as it did, Liz then hit the gas again. She powered through the vehicle by first steering right with a quick cut left then right again, leaving the SUV spinning in the middle of the road. Liz thought to herself, *let's see how they deal with that*, and accelerated away, knowing her father would be proud of her perfect pit maneuver. Sam asked, "You think that will end it, honey?" Liz glanced in her rearview mirror and replied, "We will see."

The suburban did a three-sixty as it was engulfed in smoke from its tires and slammed into the embankment on the side of the road with the front bumper stuck into the dirt. The driver threw the Suburban into reverse, which pulled the front bumper loose from the vehicle. He swerved around it and headed after Liz and Sam.

As the vehicle turned, the bumper fell off. They had to drive over the part as they accelerated after Liz and Sam. The front grill was busted now; the fender was loose and flapping in the wind. The driver had just been shown up by a little girl, and his pride couldn't handle that. With a determined expression, he jetted after her to teach her a lesson.

The attacker wasn't giving up. Liz had earned at least a mile lead and was now attempting to maintain the legal speed limit when she saw the attacker coming. She looked over at her mother and asked, "How are you doing?"

Sam gave her daughter a hard glance, trying not to sound like a whiner. "I'm doing fine, why?" Liz replied, "Well, hold on to your knickers! He is coming again." Sam whispered, "O-shit!"

Sam looked at her daughter and shook her head. Liz was thinking, *these guys don't know when to call it quits.* She forced them off the road once and pulled a pit maneuver on them, but now they were coming back.

Liz decided that she had to end this once and for all

www.ingramcontent.com/pod-product-compliance
Lightning Source LLC
LaVergne TN
LVHW040143080526
838202LV00042B/3002